Florian Barbara Gunn

Florian's Husband

In three volumes. Vol. 1

SALZWASSER
VERLAG

Florian Barbara Gunn

Florian's Husband

In three volumes. Vol. 1

Reprint of the original, first published in 1863.

1st Edition 2022 | ISBN: 978-3-37500-687-7

Verlag (Publisher): Salzwasser Verlag GmbH, Zeilweg 44, 60439 Frankfurt, Deutschland
Vertretungsberechtigt (Authorized to represent): E. Roepke, Zeilweg 44, 60439 Frankfurt, Deutschland
Druck (Print): Books on Demand GmbH, In de Tarpen 42, 22848 Norderstedt, Deutschland

FLORIAN'S HUSBAND.

FLORIAN'S HUSBAND.

"She shines—where'er I turn mine eye—
The Morning-star of Memory."

. . . .

"A shrivelled scroll, a scattered leaf."

BYRON.

IN THREE VOLUMES.

VOL. I.

LONDON

1863.

BOOK THE FIRST.

ALBERT BERANGER.

FLORIAN'S HUSBAND.

CHAPTER I.

I BEGIN TO OPEN THE WORLD'S OYSTER.—AN USHER. —OXFORD FRIENDS.—LOVE; THE DREAM.

"There's a divinity that shapes our ends."
Shakspeare.

I, GERALD GESSLER, take upon myself the dignity of HISTORIAN; not the historian of great names and glorious deeds, but of one young and simple life. I merely bare the rude thread of my own life, because it passed through the bright and beautiful fibres of other lives. This tale is truth; for be it known that I never possessed either poetry or imagination enough to invent a falsehood, far less to compose a fiction; therefore, if my tale halt, look to truth and fact for the lameness, not to fiction and fancy.

I never knew father or mother even by tradition, for they had passed away ere I knew what death was, and left neither old friend nor vassal to beguile the soft hours of twilight with the story of their good or evil.

> "To live in hearts we leave behind
> Is not to *die!*"

But surely to die in hearts we leave behind is never to have lived. This blank feeling of vague and desolate tenderness was all I ever knew of a father's and a mother's love.

They indeed left one (I will not say friend) who must have known something of them, as he was my guardian; he paid for my University and other expenses; but I never made inquiries on this subject to him. His letters to me, four in the year, enclosing a cheque for my quarterly allowance, and requesting an acknowledgment for the sum received, displayed so much cold, business-like indifference to everything connected with me, that I knew he had nothing to do with memory, wistful (I had almost written melancholy), exquisite, and holy pleasure as it is to anyone that can remember and love in the present those whom he has left in the past. This man's letters might have been taken for a study in arithmetic, for they began like a ledger and ended like a bill. I never could discover his name, for his large black heavy signature always stood obscurely mysterious at the end of his epistles, like the handwriting on Belshazzar's palace walls. I used to imitate the jumble as closely as possible, when I addressed my receipts, and my letters generally reached him.

I was a favourite with my college chums, because I never strove for, and, therefore, my vanity would whisper, never won, the prizes or honours. I was not that solitary, eccentric, and sometimes irascible thing,—a genius; nor that insolent and arrogant individual,—a "person of talent." I was a social and commonplace animal, who plodded over the poetry of the ancients as if it were a great mental quagmire that we were well out of, because it was very uncomfortable while we were in it. I never could see the wit of Horace, nor was I melted by the tenderness of Virgil, or stirred by the fire of Cicero and Homer. In fact, I always thought the compositions of these celebrities were dull reading, and that they could much more easily be made better than worse.

This matter-of-fact insensibility was a cause of sorrow to me too. I used to look with envy and wonder on the men of my college, who could feel more keen rapture in gazing on a picture or statue, or in hearing a splendid strain of fine poetry and music, than I ever experienced in the torpid happiness of a whole lifetime. My prosaic nature could not feel the pleasures of Imagination or Memory; but Hope,—that is more tangible and living than either,—in my separation from the Past, joined me to the Future. I did not own a grave on the wide earth, nor owe a tear. How happy is prose, after all! As for my personal qualifications, my features and aspect had the merit of being respectable. I think a court of law, had any sucking Lavaters been on the jury, would have acquitted me on the evidence of my general appearance; for villany requires a certain amount of intellect or cleverness, which my physiognomy did not by any means betoken. I was perfectly satisfied with my external man. This last statement may look like vanity, but it does not deserve the name, it is merely contentment; for the individual who does not possess enough of vanity to be satisfied with himself is only one remove from a misanthrope.

I shall introduce no character or incident here but those which are closely connected with the tale which I am about to tell. I premise this to excuse the following short adventure, that might otherwise appear trivial and out of place.

I had a habit in Oxford, which at that time was the sole sentimentalism of my life, of strolling away to a wood in the suburbs, at morning, noon, and twilight, there, beyond the dear old walls of the grey city, to watch the effects of sunshine and of sunset. Then I would take a book, and throwing myself down on the grass, amid the wild flowers, the dew, and the grasshoppers, would muse or read for hours, while the shadows deepened and the warm breath of the summer wind would sough sweetly through the quivering leaves. One day, many years before the time my story begins, I met a young lady in this wood—a fair, lovely botanist, with "her slight fingers full of leaves and flowers." Her violets fell as she attempted to get over the stile. I hastened forward, picked up the flowers, and helped the lady to the other side. She thanked me both with her tones and with her looks. I leant on the stile, and watched her yearningly until she disappeared down the sunny road, as if I could have called her back. I ran after her. I pray you spare your sneers, for dreamy youth at such times feels ever lonely. I claimed her as if she were a part of mine or me. I cannot define a feeling for which there is neither definition nor reason. All have experienced the uncontrollable impulse of their own emotions—a sort of insanity sometimes seizing the heart, while the mind and brain are sound.

I met her after this almost daily for years; and never without those looks which need no words to express the emotions of the heart, for it is not only a Siddons, a Kemble, or a Kean that can make silence eloquent.

This woman filled my whole soul. Love thought her beautiful, and imagined her perfect. I dreamed of her perpetually, and until this hour her image has stood between me and every other love. She came to me day after day. As she passed, I would not for worlds have lost a motion of her hand, or a rustle of her garments. I was a fool, but my folly was joy and transport to me. In my moments of reason I smiled at the feeling as evanescent first love; as a thing that would pass away for ever when the bubbles of romance my lover's fancy wrought would burst, and mingle with the base and beggarly elements of common feelings. Years and years after, I tell you to beware: first love—dream love, mad love, if you will,—anything that *is* love, is more immortal than you think. My course of study in the old University of Oxford was finished; the time came which made me lord of myself,—that heritage of woe,—and I do not think I was an hour legally more than an infant, when a miniature ledger came from my guardian, telling me, in as few words and as many figures as possible, that as I was now a man and a scholar, and a poor one to boot, without a profession, and heir only to that aforementioned noble inheritance, viz. myself,—I was now to "open the world's oyster," not with a sword, but a Latin grammar. In other words I was to be a tutor, or any other thing I pleased, for his guardianship and remittances would now cease.

This letter contained a cheque for five hundred pounds. I wrote him my last receipt, politely soliciting him for his name, but no reply ever came to this letter. Then I left the University, amid the regret and envy of a legion of college chums, and took delightful apartments in a pretty little cottage, with a trim garden and a quaint old porch, around which the honeysuckle twined in perfumed festoons. On my shelves might have been found the works of wellnigh every known poet. The cottage lay directly in the road on which my unknown beloved one passed every day. I generally sat with my parlour window wide open, dreamily drinking in the fragrance exhaled from my garden flowers, and the rapture inspired by her passing presence. I would not even put panes of thin transparent glass between my love's glances and me. It was at this period of my life that my thorough knowledge of the names and language of flowers was acquired. I was weak enough, too, to purchase a guitar and an album, also a double-barrelled opera-glass; by the use of which I was able to bring my Dulcinea as it were into my arms. I entertained my chums with choice suppers, and one evening, as I had reason to believe some of them knew who the lady was, I screwed my courage to the strongest, and gently extracted from them the name and parentage of my beloved. She was the only daughter of a Colonel Ryder, a retired officer, living in Ivy-nook Cottage, situated on the outskirts of the town; his eldest son was in the army, and his second, a deformed invalid boy, scarcely left the house, and was lovingly tended by his sister.

The Colonel gambled and betted, and as he had no funds except his pension, was known to be in debt. These gentlemanly debts of honour which become a fine gentleman, although conferring a certain distinction which common liabilities lack, still require to be liquidated, like the tradesmen's bills of of men of coarser clay. The Colonel's income, then, being insufficient, signs of proud poverty became apparent; some of the few domestics were dismissed, and tradesmen refused to transact any further business with the Ryders.

The Colonel was perhaps one of the haughtiest men in England, of a stiff, stately presence, and with an old-world dignity which, at rare times, when he chose to unbend himself, reminded one of worthy Sir Charles Grandison, of bygone fiction. His inbred *hauteur* was, moreover, by no means diminished by his sense of poverty, and altogether he was a man who, so far as externals went, while enforcing one's respect, would never have converted that feeling into aught warmer in a superficial observer. But Miss Ryder, my beloved, was one of the angels of Oxford. Wherever illness, sorrow, or misfortune was, there at their heels, before the physician or the priest—recognized by her large sun-hat—came Miss Ryder, with her little basket; the Angel of Mercy only could reach the dying and despairing before her. There was not even a sick flower or a wounded bird in Oxford, that she would not have lovingly tended. She was the "Beggar's Saint," the "Angel of the Poor."

I used to saunter past Ivy-nook Cottage every day, in the hope of obtaining one glance from those soft eyes. Was it fate, coincidence, chance, or design, that I should happen to see her on each of these occasions either on the road, or in her own garden, or at her own cottage windows? Need I say what delight it was to me to count even her glances over and over again? Need I say how her very smile was treasured up in memory's store-house as the most precious guerdon of each day's existence? It is but the old, old tale that I am telling; old as the balmy summer days when Adam and Eve, as yet uncursed, walked through the glades of Eden. Blessed are my recollections of my love's young dream. I would dream it yet again to-night!

My days of mental labour and study I felt were over for ever. Love ruins man as a student. It may help the soldier to gain his feverish glory, and the dreaming poet his flimsy fame, but I was neither; and sitting down in the midst of my glorious infatuation, I threw away my books, and hugged my ideal to my heart of hearts.

There was an undergraduate of Christ Church, for whom I entertained a *soi-disant* friendship; his name was Sheridan Hope, generally called Sherry by his friends. Gifted with wondrous physical advantages, added to singularly fascinating manners, his sentiments, nevertheless, were very objectionable, and his morals doubtful. He was guilty of many foolish and questionable acts; yet, his fund of animal spirits being so exuberant, his wit so sparkling and withal so worldly-wise and practical, everybody liked him; in fact, Sherry Hope was a very popular young man. He swore by his honour, yet often acted in a manner which showed he was not guided by it.

I was standing by the stile one afternoon—

dreaming of that day's looks—when Sherry came up, and greeting me with a hearty clap on the back:—

"You have left college," said he; "in earnest?"

"Yes," replied I; "do you think I have done so too soon?"

"Not I, old fellow. But what do you mean to do? To live on your fortune, eh?"

"I have no fortune to live on," replied I.

"The deuce!" exclaimed he, "haven't you? That is a miserable prospect for a man who is constitutionally lazy."

"I am not constitutionally lazy," said I, starting and blushing.

"Your behaviour belies you then, for you look and act devilishly like it!" cried he, striking his boots with his golden-headed cane. "The men here all remark your idle, meaningless saunters, and call you all manner of queer names."

This was a dreadful shock to me. Was this the reputation I had gained in Oxford, where Miss Ryder lived?

"I'm to leave Oxford next week," cried I,

with a melancholy look in the direction of Ivy-nook Cottage. This statement was made on the nonce.

"Where for?" inquired Sherry.

"London," answered I, at random again.

"Ah! a glorious place. What will you do then?"

"Live on my own exertions," replied I.

"As you haven't a profession, I suppose that means being a tutor or pedagogue," said he.

"A tutor," replied I, drily and curtly.

"In what family? I know several 'crack' families in London."

"I do not know yet."

"Ah! you'll advertise in *The Times*, or answer the advertisements, and get or beg letters of introduction. I can give you one, but it is to a gentleman who keeps a cockpit."

"Thank you; I'll not trouble you for it," replied I.

"I also know," he continued, "a brace or two of military men, fellows in the Line. My chief chum is in the Buffs; he is a man from Oxford. If you would like an introduction to him, I would——"

"A thousand thanks, Sherry," replied I, absently. "But I don't go to London for gaiety and champagne suppers."

Had I but known at that time who this military friend was!

This conversation suggested my future course to me; I would go to London, and advertise in *The Times*. What other course was open to me? I accordingly made arrangements for my departure, and after they were completed, went a round of farewell visits. As many of them were to casual acquaintances, or people who had no connection with the story I am about to narrate, I will pass these over.

I paid a visit to Major Marr, a gentleman with whom, till then, I was not personally acquainted, and had only seen in the streets. I had a slight intimacy with his son Philip, who after taking degrees in the University, had gone to study law in a solicitor's office in London. He was many years my senior, and had finished his curriculum shortly after my "coming up." He was a reserved and intellectual man; one could love, respect, and place all confidence in, yet never be familiar with him. He passed his final examination with great *éclat.* There was no stain on his moral character, and in intelligence he surpassed every student in the University. If he was calm, quiet, and unexcitable, it was because he could restrain the strong passions of his nature. I have heard him read vehement passages from Shakespeare and Byron, with a fire and power of expression really wonderful. His elocution was marvellous; but it was that of a reader, not of an actor.

I had esteemed and loved this almost stranger, and I now went to his father to obtain his address in London. The Major's dwelling was an exquisite little cottage, with snowy walls, snowy curtains, white railings, balconies, and window sills; but the universal whiteness was brilliantly relieved by scarlet runners, crimson fuchsias, china roses, and all manner of red-tinted flowers, which sprung everywhere like flames of fire. Two little silky spaniels played on the gravel, pretty enough to remind me of Landseer's picture of Vernon's pet dogs. I was coaxing the tiny black fellow to come to me through the rails, when a young rich voice cried, in a tone of command not to be disobeyed,

"How dare you, Witch? come back!"

The obedient creature crept away from the gate, and lay down at the feet of a lovely and dashing brunette, who came forward and fixed me with a large dark eye that flashed like a sword-blade.

"Pray, does Major Marr reside here?" said I.

She advanced nearer, and caressing her plump white arms looked up in my face. What a fiery, changing expression she had! Even the bright black eyes, with their piercing glance, seemed to deepen or soften in hue with the feeling of the moment. The bloom on her cheeks was changeful too, for their blush came and went perpetually. The small head was crowned with masses of jet black hair, tossing and waving like a silken banner in a brisk gale. The delicate hands were never at rest, and even the soft shoulder shrugged itself bewitchingly. Taken all in all, she was a beautiful and striking being.

"Yes," replied she, opening the gate.

"Papa is at home, come in." I followed her and the two spaniels into a plain but cheerful breakfast parlour which looked into the garden. The furniture of the chamber was antique, and a few yellow old-fashioned military pictures adorned the walls. The Major soon after came puffing in, in the easy undress of a blue jacket and a straw hat. He started and bowed hastily.

"Bless me, Eagle!" cried he, "why did you not tell me there was a stranger here? Have a seat, sir. Pray excuse my attire, I am an inveterate gardener. Be seated."

"Eagle!" thought I, "what a name for a young lady! But then her heavy black curls have the flap of glossy wings about them."

The Major's appearance, even had he been dressed in the full dignity of uniform, was not of the imposing and majestic type: he was small and stout, with a large head and a broad chest; but his features and voice betrayed dry humour and great warmth of heart. He was better than dignified, he was genial. When he learned the object of my visit he became rather perplexed, and assumed such a manner that I feared I had unwittingly offended him.

"Philip would not enter the army," said he. "He had the offer of a commission in a cavalry regiment, but refused it; he is of a grave and studious disposition as you know, and has talents of a very high order; his inclinations pointed to the bar, and as we are not so wealthy and influential now as the Marrs have been, my son had to fill an inferior position (very far beneath his intellect and birth) in a solicitor's office."

After this explanation of what I believe was the cause of his embarrassment, the Major laid aside his dignity and became genial again.

"Mr. Marr will be himself in any position," answered I. "His genius and rectitude will honour every place, and make every place honour him."

"I cannot affect to deny it, sir," cried the Major. "He is not a soldier, but curse me (excuse me, sir, we sometimes used to swear a little in the army), he is as brave a man as ever stood before or behind a cannon!"

"Not so brave as Jack Brown, of 'Ours,' Papa, is he?" archly cried Miss Eagle.

"Every bit, you minx," cried the Major, stroking her glossy black hair. "It's not every man that can say he won or defended colours at Waterloo; and when we were at Brussels——"

"Don't go to Brussels to-day, Papa," said merry Eagle, "it is too far away!"

The Major's eyes twinkled with fun.

"Well, well," said he, "it was no story, only an incident of the War. Jack Brown was the handsomest and finest fellow in the whole regiment, and even now retains——"

"Oh! Papa, he has only one leg, one eye, he wears a wig, and uses snuff!" laughed Eagle. "I wish you could only see this Apollo of the 4th, Mr. Gessler."

"There are the women, sir," cried the Major, "laughing at us again; there was a minx something like Eagle in Brussels, and——"

"You're away again, Papa," cried Eagle. "Good-bye! good-bye!"

"I give Waterloo up, sir," cried the Major.

"The battle is over for this day. Did you see my geraniums outside, sir? They will excuse my undress."

We went into the garden.

"Keep your puppies from the flowers, Eagle; that little devil Wizard has a habit of tearing up the beds with his paws, and Witch rolls herself in the mignonette."

The young lady took the spaniels in her arms. Small wonder, thought I, that she has so much magic about her, when a Witch and a Wizard are her daily companions. After a long saunter through the delightful garden, and some more conversation on different subjects, I bid farewell to the Major and his daughter. At parting the old gentleman said,—

"You will catch the last few months of Phil's celibacy; he is to marry very shortly the loveliest and the sweetest girl in England. Don't pout, Eagle; ladies are so jealous of each other, Mr. Gessler, it is quite awful."

"We are only jealous of Waterloo heroes, Papa, and the officers of the 4th," said Eagle, wickedly swinging her curls.

I was made the bearer of a small box to Mr. Marr, containing sundry cakes, preserves, and poultry, all gifts from the old housekeeper. Miss Eagle's parting words were :—

"I know, Papa, that Phil would like a few flowers from our own garden, and that he would value them more than Mrs. Richards' chickens and jellies. And as Mr. Gessler does not leave till to-morrow afternoon, Florian and I will have a bouquet ready to send him, of half-blown flowers, that will not cast their leaves, or open, till they get to London."

"I shall be delighted to carry them," said I.

"And tell him, Mr. Gessler," continued she, earnestly, "that Florian has not forgotten him, for Phil is very much afraid of woman's forgetfulness, as he calls it; and I have to write away this fear in every letter I send him. Tell him, too, that Witch and Wizard are well, and that the hair has grown beautifully again on Witch where it had been burned. Tell him, also,—but perhaps you will not remember all that I have been saying?" She paused and shook her plumage like a very Eagle.

"I'm certain I'll recollect every word of it," replied I, warmly.

"Perhaps you cannot," said she. "But you will remember that about Florian, wont you? What you say about Florian will be as sweet to him as the flowers you bring with you. It will be cruel of you to forget either; for spoken words satisfy more than written ones, and I want Phil to be satisfied about Florian." She ended her words with a blush.

"That is one of Eagle's speeches, sir," cried the Major, with twinkling eyes. "If you, a stranger, understand it, I give you credit for genius, sir. It merely means that Florian loves Phil yet; that's what the oracle means to say, sir."

The old gentleman evidently wished to be sharply witty and dreadfully satirical.

"I understood it so myself, Major," said I. "I shall not lose a word on my journey: the sayings of oracles should be treasured, you know."

"You'll look in here when you come back to Oxford," said the Major, "and as you will see poor Phil, you will tell us all about him.

I should have said, if you please, and I'll feel obliged; but hang it, sir, we Waterloo men, like Othello, are not accustomed to the 'set phrase of speech.' Is that a proper quotation, Eagle?"

My next farewell visit was to one of the most eccentric men in Oxford. There was an old dark house, enclosed within high black walls, on the outskirts of the town, which I often passed in my walks. A light, which always burned in one of the topmost windows, excited my curiosity, and I frequently used to peer in at the small iron gate; but never beheld anything but the quaint old garden, with its singular adornments of awning and coloured lamps. A tall, elderly man, rather clerically dressed, with a pouch slung on his back, was sometimes seen in the streets of Oxford and its neighbourhood; he frequently went into apothecaries' shops, but was oftener seen in the fields and woods searching for weeds and herbs. I used to observe him attentively; and, from his thoughtful stoop and the paleness of his visage, I regarded him as a solitary monomaniac of science. On inquiring who he was, I learned that he called himself an herbalist and chemist, but was thought to be a half-insane alchemist, searching for the philosopher's stone and the elixir of life.

At a casual glance he appeared to have a calm, passionless face, whereon thought (or one thought) was perpetually written. His manner was that of a man ever in a state of abstraction; although he looked at me, he did not seem to see me. One day I saw him in a long grey dressing-gown, tending some flowers in his garden. I became acquainted with him in this way—As he was passing me on the road one morning, he accidentally dropped some herbs, which I picked up and returned to him. As we walked on, we entered into conversation. He invited me into his house to see his laboratory, and I frequently availed myself of the invitation. We cannot help feeling an interest in eccentricity, and, even when it appears allied to madness, we worship genius. My friend, Dr. Castellon, had genius, but he unfortunately entertained dogmas which shut him out from fame; he despised contemporary and raved about posthumous glory and appreciation; and in all likelihood his desire would be gratified: the mountain of renown does not come to man, but man must go to the mountain.

I found Dr. Castellon in his laboratory, working among his stores, drugs, and herbs. When I told him my intention of leaving Oxford, he appeared surprised, and, leaning on a pestle, thoughtfully and almost sadly, he said,—"You are going out into the world. You will go among men, and be the companion of thousands. I envy you the book you are about to read—Human Nature. I envy you the brothers and sisters you will find among men and women, the passions you will feel, the friendships you will make, the things you will love, and the things you will seek, whether you can obtain them or not. Human passions and energies should not run to waste, and die unused, as many of mine have wasted and died. We are born to wrestle and subdue, to suffer and enjoy, and not to curdle and chill, or whiten like snow, and then melt away. I envy you at this moment, and regret myself."

"Your envy and regret are both misplaced," said I.

"You do not understand me," replied he. "The misery of old age, and of that toil which after all is only sloth, is on me now. Better I had used my ovens to bake bread than to cook drugs. I think this sometimes, I think so now. But come, and let me teach you your last lesson in analysis."

Then I beheld the magic and necromancy of science,—chemistry at work. Dr. Castellon named it the play of philosophy, for it is an absorbing and bewitching occupation. We forgot the world, till darkness began to gather over our crucibles. Then I expressed a desire to go below, to bid farewell to Madame Castellon and her daughter, for the chemist was a Benedict. The Castellons were Spanish, but the cast of Madame Castellon's features was half-Turkish and half-Jewish. The type is common but striking, and often beautiful. In this case it only struck, and did not charm, for the lineaments were too prominent, and the expression hard and austere. Her eyes were soft and languid, though in conversation they sometimes appeared keen and ardent. The voice was soft and deep, and she spoke English with a peculiar intonation, continually faltering over Saxon words, as soft feet stumble over stones. She always was attired with great simplicity, but the rich Asiatic character of her face and voice made her plain garments appear as if they were only a disguise. She was a strange woman, and as it appeared to me, must have experienced great changes in the course of her life. Passionate and impulsive, at times she seldom spoke, at other times she was very voluble.

When I descended, I found her and her daughter sitting at the open window of the small sitting-room on the ground floor. The elder lady appeared to be sewing; but as it was almost twilight, she must have had an eagle's eye to stitch cambric in such a gloom. But madame's work was often an excuse for silence; I frequently imagined so, and it seemed so now. Her daughter Kilda came forward and met me, looking so white and lovely as she issued from the shadows, that she reminded me of a lily breaking out in the midst of ivy. Kilda resembled that style of lady whom Vandyck delighted to paint. She was attired in a dark, close-fitting dress, buttoned at the neck and wrists; her black hair was drawn back from her face, and hidden behind in sable lace and velvet, so that her pale, beautiful countenance, and exquisitely delicate throat and hands, with their pure rich cool tints, stood out in clear and charming relief. How the mother and daughter resembled one another!—the daughter like the leaf of some tree in June, young and green; the mother the same leaf in September, old and sere.

When I first knew Miss Castellon, her knowledge of the English language was very imperfect. Although I was not her teacher, she had a habit of making me explain any word I used which was not intelligible to her. Madame Castellon did not seem to hear or see me when I sat down beside her.

"You are always at work, madame," said I. "You are more industrious than the bees, for they do not gather their honey in the evening, I believe."

"I do nothing," said she, stiffly. "The bees toil, but I only trifle. I thought you were not alone when you entered."

"I was quite alone, madame," answered I.

"Madame!" repeated Miss Castellon, sharply, in her foreign-sounding English, "Madame! what does that mean?"

"It is a form of address to a lady," replied I, "a term of respect and courtesy."

"It is dark at last," said madame, laying down her cambric, with a sigh. "Close the window and light the lamp; we do not know what may come to us in the darkness; there is not a light anywhere up or down. Do you hear me, Kilda?"

I closed the casement, and told them of my departure next morning for London. Kilda placed her hand on my arm.

"Mother," said she, "do not light the lamps; Mr. Gessler is going to bid us farewell."

"Indeed!" exclaimed Madame Castellon, hastening to the fireside, and sewing by the firelight. "Indeed! you will feel happy."

"No, he does not," cried Kilda, "he is leaving friends to go among strangers."

"Strangers will never wrong or injure him, child, but friends will," said madame. "Dr. Castellon holds another opinion, but I am unshaken in mine; I could tell you tales of what friends have done to friends that would make you tremble, but I will not. You say you go to London to be a tutor; there will lie a deep responsibility on you, sir. You will have the first handling of fresh young minds; I hope your hands will be clean and white ere you touch them."

Madame spoke in a low, deep voice, sitting by the fire-side, but she never raised her eyes, but continued to stitch quietly and blindly.

"I will try and keep them pure and unsoiled," said I; speaking as she had spoken, figuratively. Kilda, who had been silent, came from the window, and we three stood on the hearth; she looked as lovely and witch-like as a beautiful woman always looks with darkness around her and the fire-light on her face.

"Friend!" she mused, in a dreamy voice. "I know what a friend is; it has the same exquisite meaning as lover. I have no friends. I had none yesterday, I have none to-day. I shall have none to-morrow. I neither remember nor anticipate any."

"How often do I tell you that it is fortunate to be so situated?" said her mother, sharply. "Is my experience nothing? Psha! it has snapped in two." And she threw a glittering needle among the flames.

Miss Castellon did not reply but said after a pause, "You are going away to learn the world's wicked philosophy; when you return you will be a learned old cynic, incapable of feeling a warm passion even if you would. My father showed me an acid, or was it a gas, that gave a great brilliancy to everything that came near it, but at the same time consumed everything. Do you not understand the comparison, Mr. Gessler? You are going into the world; you will experience its influence; you may become a man of polished manners, celebrated for your wit and wisdom, but when I see you again (if I ever see you), your heart will be gone, cankered away by this terrible moral gas. You can only save it by giving it to these poor unlettered preservers of hearts—women! Oh! leave your heart with one of us till you return."

Was this banter or earnest? I know not, I was not calm enough to discover; for Miss Ryder's memory filled the room like a sunbeam, or was it like a shadow? I muttered some husky words, I know not what they were.

"I thank you, Mr. Gessler, for one thing," said Kilda, "I never saw a man before who, when woman's foolish and faithful love was mentioned, remained serious, and even displayed emotion. You have my gratitude."

There was something touching in her words, looks, and tones.

I rose to depart. Madame gave me a long keen look over her cambric; held out her hand, and muttering "Good-bye," applied herself to her interminable seam again. Kilda came out with me to the garden.

"Do you know," said she, "that I expect misfortune and sorrow; for a strange thing, like an omen or a prophecy, occurred to-day. I found some flowers, which were fresh and blooming last night, shrivelled and black."

She led me to a bed of flowers; and there I beheld a cluster of amaranths, faded and dead, as if in mockery of that immortality of which they are said to be an emblem.

"And you are leaving us to-morrow?" cried she. "Look, our very flowers lament and die for you."

I smiled, and shook my head.

"If you would only be taught and not teach," exclaimed she, "if you would only remain here. Pray do, for her sake, for somebody's sake, not for mine; for I am nothing to any one, desolate, unloved, and unloving as I am. Do not go."

Woman's beauty is powerful, but love for woman is more powerful still. Kilda's presence was not so potent as Miss Ryder's absence; the living presence of the lovely was nothing in comparison with the pale and distant shadow of the loved. Moore has written a simple and pretty line,

"To love is not so sweet as to remember thee, Mary,"

expressing my meaning more beautifully than I could myself.

"I am poor, Miss Castellon," said I. "I have something to do in the world, and must do it. Necessity drives me away, and I *must* go."

"Then come back again," said she, "come back soon; the feelings of our hearts were never given to be wasted in lonely monotonous study. Come back soon."

"Beauty is a tyrant," saith Socrates—a short-lived tyranny, the brief despotism of a flower or a butterfly; the Nero of a month, and sometimes of a minute. Promising to correspond with Miss Castellon, and to see her soon again, I then bade her farewell.

My next visit was to the most desolate man in Oxford. Mr. Pietro Wells was Greek master in a boys' school; the most wretched of that wretched class—under-ushers. To make the under-usher of a noisy boys' school the most miserable of created beings, it only requires him to be a gentleman, and a book-worm of quiet, studious habits; and my wan, attenuated, and patched friend was both. He was very tall, and, to use a common expression, as thin as a shadow. He was so pale, that some of the undergraduates doubted if he had any blood. His Roman features were keen and sharp, and his eyes large and glassy, never evincing the slightest feeling. He was the butt of ridicule to the school-boys, but he appeared insensible to all their gibes and jests. I used to see him every day, at the play-hour, sitting on a door-step of the school, in his accustomed posture; his angular elbows resting on his equally angular knees, his yellow skeleton hands supporting his lank pale cheeks, his book on his lap, and his long grey hair waving over it. He always seemed so absorbed in his book, that he was apparently unconscious of all that happened around him. On one particular day, the young gentlemen determined to try the scholarly abstraction of Pietro Wells, by sending down on him, from a window above where he sat, a shower of mimic rain. I was passing at the time, and observed the trick at once. The poor usher, supposing the shower really came from the clouds of heaven, pulled up his superannuated coat-collar and read on. By some means or other I made the boys desist, never imagining that the absent book-worm knew anything about it; but that same night he came and thanked me, and from that day we were friends. Indeed, while I remained in Oxford, he received more of my guardian's quarterly instalments than I did myself, for I had few uses for money. I also saved him from many annoyances and practical jokes. His home was a very humble one, a small "three-pair back" apartment, in a narrow lane, a short distance from my college, where, generally with some gift, I frequently visited him. To be treated like a Christian, especially by an undergraduate, was something wonderful to Pietro Wells. This being my last night in Oxford, I stole out, bearing my parting gift, to bid him farewell. His salary, small though it was, would have been adequate for his few wants, if he had had no mania for old books and MSS.; but each man has his own temptation, which he is unable and unwilling to resist, and this was the weakness of Pietro Wells. I entered the narrow dark lane, lit only by a few lamps, and, plunging into its

Cimmerian gloom, ascended the high wooden staircase. I knocked at the door of his small dark room, and after a long pause, and another knock, his low, hollow voice said, "Come in." He was sitting on a straw chair by a smouldering fire. A rushlight guttered and flickered in a rude candlestick, by the yellow dismal light of which he looked at least sixty, and old even for that age. Study, mental anxiety, and physical toil, poverty and sorrow, and not time—for Pietro was only a few years over forty—had aged him. It was easy to see that his was the old age, not of years, but of misfortune.

CHAPTER II.

TWO OTHER FAREWELLS.—LONDON.—MR. ALBERT BERANGER.—PHILIP MARR.

"The world was all before me where to choose."
Milton.

WITH the instinct of hospitality Pietro trimmed the dim fire as I entered, and offered me a chair, his eye sparkling with a light suggestive of the gratification with which he received me.

"Mr. Gessler," said he, "I am glad to see you, very glad; you are as welcome as if you were——"

This simile was one which, although he frequently began it, he never ended. I often thought he might have meant "Death."

"It is a clear moonlight night, Mr. Wells," I exclaimed.

"Is it?" returned he, dreamily. "I dare say, I dare say."

He then relapsed into silence. Mr. Pietro Wells was very taciturn when I visited him, but as I did not go to converse with him, but only to ruminate in his company, he seemed to enjoy it. His conversation at the best was very broken, and I had never been able to ascertain anything of his past life, except that England was not his birth-place.

A Greek book, which he had been reading, was lying on the table beside him. I often used to sit watching the pale light glimmering on his strange face, fixed in thought, listening to the wild winter winds as they rushed down the lane with a sound resembling the cry of a spirit in agony.

"This is the saddest visit I have ever paid you, Mr. Wells," said I, at last.

"Did you speak?" said he, after a long pause.

I repeated my observation, and after a dreamy silence, he said, "Why?"

"Because," returned I, "I am going away."

The muscles of his face moved as I never had seen them move before.

"Pooh!" cried he. "Everything is going away; the old University is slowly creeping away. Even *I* am going away; everything is travelling off to the grand old city—Ruin. To be 'going away' is to live. Pooh, pooh!"

"But I mean Oxford," said I. "I am leaving Oxford, Mr. Wells."

"You must leave it, you mean," answered he. "Men only do what they must do. Say that you cannot stay."

"I have told you the circumstances of my life, Mr. Wells," said I; "and by a letter which I received lately I find that my correspondent's guardianship has ceased. It is imperative for me now to leave Oxford, and become a tutor."

I thought he did not hear me, he was so long silent. At last, however, after a long pause, he said,

"Whither will you go?"

"I scarcely know," replied I. "The wide world is all before me; but I think I shall go to London—adventurers always go to London."

"London!" echoed he; "London!"

And starting up, he plunged his lank arms into an old box in a corner of the room, after he had unlocked it with some rusty keys. Taking out a packet of papers, he thrust them into the pocket of his tattered coat, at the same time bringing out writing materials, and appearing much moved and excited, as I thought, at my going away.

"I will not be long out of Oxford, Mr. Wells," said I. "Oxford is more home to me than any other place in the world. One of my best friends is in Oxford—yourself."

Pietro Wells did not weep as I said this. Much as he must have felt it, he shed no tears. His muscles worked spasmodically—the glassy eyes became distended—floods of tears could not have been more bitter.

"I never was a friend to anyone," said he; "would I were a friend! But I am only a bookworm, Mr. Gessler, and an usher—these are my only names. Friend is a title, a name of human kindred, like father, son, and brother. A friend is a brother of another blood. You cannot call me anybody's *brother!*"

"Indeed I do," said I, warmly. "I shall always think you so in my heart."

He sat down at the table, pulled out the packet from his pocket, removed layers of newspapers from it, and, spreading a part of the parchment before him on the table, wrote. I knew his large, stiff, tremulous handwriting well. It was a diffuse epistle, for he wrote very rapidly, and took a considerable time. At length he finished it, and putting it all back into the newspaper layers again, said,

"You will do me a favour, Mr. Gessler; I know you will. You are one of the very few human beings who grant favours to poverty and sorrow. You will grow more like your species when you get older; however, you will do this now, for you cannot become old and diseased in heart in one day, even although you breathe the air infected by mankind. You will do this?"

"On condition of your granting me a favour in return, Mr. Wells," said I.

"I do promise," replied he, "if I give you pleasure by so doing. I never saw such a marvellous being as you."

After saying this he began to stare at me as before, but I at once interrupted him, saying,

"I thank you for your kind concession, Mr. Wells; what is the favour you desire me to grant?"

"To deliver this letter and packet to the address," returned he, giving them to me. The direction was "Mr. Albert Beranger, 10, Blank Street, London." I assured him that I would do so punctually on my arrival there.

"Yes," responded he, musingly. "Deliver them immediately, it will be better; nay, best."

"I shall write to you, Mr. Wells," said I, preparing to go. "That is, if you will care to hear from me. And if you will answer me sometimes, only sometimes, Mr. Wells——"

"You will hear of me, Mr. Gessler," replied he, "even if you do not hear from me; but I will write to you sometimes. I shall be glad to hear from you, too," he continued. "Yes, I will even be glad. I shall feel the strange, old, half-forgotten feeling of gladness once more when I read your letters. I know you will write for this cause, when you remember it; but it is so natural to forget anything like me in the great world. But I forgive you beforehand for your forgetfulness. I shall love and bless you, Mr. Gessler, while I have life, for what you have been; I care not for what you will be. If there is no oblivion for the woe and evil of the past, there is also none for its joy and gladness. I like to think of that."

"A thousand thanks, Mr. Wells," said I giving him the grasp of farewell. "You do not know how sorry I am to leave Oxford, because you are in it. This is one of the most sorrowful farewells of my life. I part from one I love. Have you no advice to give me, Mr. Wells?"

"Yes," said he. "This. Cling to that which many scoff at—Virtue. Cultivate and trust everything that strengthens this virtue, even although it should be a superstition or a dream. Virtue makes as bright a heaven on earth as the Heaven which Religion pictures. Virtue is never cheated out of a heaven—remember that. You are not a genius, Mr.

Gessler; but be ambitious, and great without it. Genius is an accursed and miserable gift —a graveyard light, that only glorifies a tomb and a name; its joys are fevers, its sorrows hells. Better to be great without genius!"

I started, and the blood poured in streams of fire through my veins. "Great without genius!" The old usher of Oxford had spoken the text of which my life was to be the sermon. "Great without genius!" How many voiceless things throughout my life echoed these words to me!

Our farewell was silent after that. He gave me as a *souvenir* an old edition of "Sophocles," the first book he laid his hand on. I pressed my gift into his hand, and stumbled out. The winds on that dark night, as I went down the familiar lane, gazing back at the obscure glimmer in Pietro Wells' window, moaned out to me a farewell of their own. And every well known place and thing which the moonbeam lighted on, even the rustling of the leaves, the scents of trees and shrubs, seemed to me like voices softly saying, "Farewell."

I then went to Ivynook Cottage. The white curtains were drawn down, and there was no sound but that caused by swinging of the branches, and the bark of a distant watch dog, I plucked some flowers nearest me, in the hope that Miss Ryder's hand might have touched them.

Walking slowly round to the back of the house, I beheld the interior of a chamber, the curtains of which were only partially drawn down. The blood rushed through my veins, all my pulses beat with excitement; but, without explaining what I felt, I will tell what I saw. The apartment was a small breakfast parlour, with a couch at one side, on which a boy lay sleeping. Miss Ryder sat beside him, like a ministering angel. As the boy seemed restless and feverish, she was laying damp white napkins on his hot brow as he slumbered. They were alone together; and I had a long stolen gaze at her. Is it theft to steal a look? Is it impertinent and intrusive to pilfer a glance at anything sacred? To hide, and worship in secret? What delight it was to behold her, even although leagues should separate us before to-morrow's sun went down. She was sitting, half in the light and half in the shadow, a braid of her beautiful hair falling on her darkened cheeks. Her soft blue eyes lay in the shade like violets under leaves. I knew by her unclosed red lips,—like pinks blushing in the sun,—what was the hidden feeling of her heart. The glance of her beautiful eye always spoke to me a language which I had no difficulty in understanding. The expression of deep love for the sleeping boy shone like the light of Paradise in her fair face. If one leaf from the future had been read to me then; if I had known at that moment what her destiny was to be—what one year would make her and me—what *her* fate would render *my* fate; if I had known anything of this, as she sat in the quiet chamber of her father's house, watching the sick slumber of her young brother, and as I, with the wet, green ivy around me, stood in the little gate, watching her, "I would have shut the book, sat down, and prayed for death." But I did not know it then, and even if I had, perhaps I would have lived on to worship her.

I stood among the dripping boughs, till the boy's feverish sleep was over, when the lamp was carried away, and the chamber remained empty.

My last morning in Oxford rose fair and gloriously; perhaps to inspire me with regret at going away, or to smile on my lonely departure into the battle-field of the world. How many students I have seen leaving Oxford with joy, hope, and transport, as captives leave their prison-house, or as creatures of the ocean plunge into their briny home again! But this was not my feeling. The adventures, the struggles, and successes of the world had no glittering lure for me, and I would fain have been the collegian for ever. I can aver with safety, that not a student in the University would believe me if I had told him this; for was it not the summit of every Oxonian's ambition, "to have done with College, and to go to London?" But I was one of the very few who did not own, on the whole earth, father, mother, brethren, kindred, home, country, or people. I could not point out my birthplace on the map of the world, nor could I have recognized the lineaments of my parents in the most faithful portraits. I was an exile, a Pariah, the Oxford Ishmael; I was poor, also, and, to close the catalogue of my misfortunes, I loved wildly, ambitiously, and hopelessly. But I do not mean to pule; I am not a silken spaniel to sit down and whine with pain, but a sulky, morose bull-dog, who gives one good growl and is done with it.

I had no time for reveries of any description, for my apartments all that morning were crowded with men of my college, bidding me farewell. I had to pledge these young gentlemen in Burgundy, which they had privately and secretly conveyed to my apartments, for the purpose of celebrating the ancient rite of the stirrup cup.

They accompanied me to the station, and favoured me with a hearty, lusty English cheer when the train started. As it glided away from the station, the last echo of the cheer died out; and old Oxford town and its venerable colleges melted from my sight.

Does mankind always hope? Is change always acceptable to the human heart? I think not; men sometimes are perfectly hopeless, and sometimes perfectly contented, I felt the latter in Oxford, and the former on leaving it. My heart swelled to bursting as the green woods flew past me, and I saw Ivynook Cottage like a small speck in the distance. The winged railway is a dreadful thing, bearing us so quickly from all we love and cherish. I soon found myself in London, and, entering the first hotel that attracted me by its blazing windows, I "turned in" and slept till morning without a dream. That day I shaved for the first time; and after my matin meal, and this rather premature operation, I sallied forth into the noisy streets. Frequently inquiring my way, and receiving conflicting directions as often, I at last arrived at Blank Street, in which was the mansion of Mr. Beranger. I rang the bell, and a lackey opened the door. To my surprise he did not run me over from head to foot with a supercilious stare; he did not even look at me at all.

"Is Mr. Beranger at home?" I inquired.

"Coffee!" said the man with a vague look and tone.

"Is he disengaged?" I interrogated again; thinking that he, like Hamlet, might be given to soliloquy.

"Ten!" said the dreamer, in the same manner as before.

"Could I see him?" said I again. "I have a packet for him."

"See!" said the liveried oracle; and taking my card he disappeared, and after the lapse of a few moments I perceived him again on a distant staircase, beckoning me in dumb show to follow. He kept out of speaking distance, and walked with an equable and stately pace; pausing at length at a door, on opening which he announced me with great dignity, and then retired.

The chamber was a library, the walls being garnished with rows of magnificent books (if literature can be judged by its binding). The ruddy reflection of a glowing fire warmed the tints of the oak and garnet furniture, against which, to use a technical expression, the white busts and statuettes "told" beautifully. Altogether it was as sumptuous an apartment as any bookworm in the world could sit down in. There was, indeed, a peculiar exciting odour pervading it, but so subtle and impalpable, that it was more perceptible to the brain than to the sense. Something like vertigo seized me as I entered, but I shook it off.

A dark, singular-looking man, of about fifty or thereabout, attired in a black velvet *dishabillé*, with a cap of the same material, was seated near the fire: his hands were nervously busy with some object that lay on the table, over which he threw a large cambric napkin. A strange undefined emotion passed through my mind as I stood in his presence for the first time. Although the atmosphere was rich and heated, I became chill and cold. Did the presentiment of all this man, Albert Beranger, would be to me and to many whom I esteemed and loved, overshadow me from the first?

The gentleman rose, and with graceful courtesy returned by bow. I took the seat he offered, and as he made an observation on the weather, I looked in his face, and saw his eye for the first time. Its expression was not that of an ordinary human being, for there was such mysterious power in its glance that I felt fascinated and enchained. It seemed to penetrate my inmost being, and read every emotion of my heart. Then, in a moment, the expression changed; the supernatural fire by which it seemed lighted up disappeared, and the look with which it remained fixed on me was calm and composed.

Everything about Mr. Beranger betokened the high-bred and courtly gentleman. In form, face, manners, and mien he was almost perfect, but as I looked at him I instinctively thought of the "gentlemanly Lucifer" of Byron's "Cain." Why such an analogy should present itself to my mind, at that time, I cannot explain. Mr. Beranger was short of stature, and slightly built; his features were elongated and fine; and his complexion was mellowed rather than bronzed by Asiatic birth and a foreign sun. His mouth was sharply cut, and its peculiar contour gave a firm expression to his face.

Although he endeavoured to assume an appearance of candour, I could not but see that it was only artifice. Whatever outward manner he might choose to assume, one could not but feel that there was something concealed beneath this external show, and it was therefore impossible to place entire confidence in him.

"Allow me to explain the cause of my intrusion," said I; "Mr. Pietro Wells, of Oxford, desired me to deliver this to you."

I rose and gave him the packet; an expression of pain was visible for a moment in his face, but it passed away in an instant.

"Mr. Pietro Wells!" he echoed, in the tone of one who associates a name with an idea. "I thank you, Mr. Gessler. May I request you to remain until I have perused these papers?"

I expressed my willingness to remain, and sat down.

Mr. Wells has probably omitted to send me his address," said he; "that is a trick of bookworms and scholars, you know, Mr.

Gessler; and a letter of this length generally requires a reply."

"Mr. Wells is seldom very diffuse either with his pen or in conversation," said I. "He seems to have been wonderfully so in this case."

"Indeed—is he not?" returned Mr. Beranger.

I could not discover by his manner whether Mr. Wells and he were friends or enemies.

"Have you been long absent from Oxford?" said he, again.

"Since yesterday," replied I. "I arrived in London last night, and have fulfilled my promise to Mr. Wells, to deliver these papers to you immediately.

Mr. Beranger made no reply. A rich golden breakfast-service lay on the table beside him, which he drew towards him, and pouring out of a delicate gold vessel some dark and fragrant coffee, he offered me one of the two cups which he had filled, saying—

"Will you have some authentic Mocha, Mr. Gessler? I always keep a coffee-cup for my friends, you see."

"They ought to feel grateful," exclaimed I,

"for it is exquisite; unrivalled in taste and perfume. This would even satisfy a Turk."

Mr. Beranger laughed—a peculiar laugh, the meaning of which I did not understand till afterwards.

"I am delighted to hear you praise it so warmly," said he; "I am an inveterate Mocha bibber, and, like all true believers, I seek to make my worship universal. This is the powerful rival of wine in Turkey, Mr. Gessler; it is because of their Mocha, and not their morality, that the Turks are the only race in the universe who have raised no altar to Bacchus. By-the-bye, did you perceive any odour when you came in? That was a Turkish importation also; nothing goes into my hookah but Turkish weed." And he drew towards him a costly and handsome oriental pipe, of ivory with gold mountings.

"Draw your chair closer to the fire, Mr. Gessler," said he; "I like a roystering fire like this, especially when it is so cold outside."

He still had the packet unopened in his hand, but he now took it up and broke the seals.

"Will you excuse me if I read this, Mr.

Gessler?" said he. "You will find 'Montaigne,' under his bust there; open the book at any place, and you will soon forget my rudeness."

The silvery tinkle of a Buhl clock striking the hour, twice warned me of the flight of time as we sat absorbed in book and parchment. But the essays of Montaigne were novel and bewitching to me, and two hours swept by before I was interrupted by the voice of my host.

"A thousand pardons, Mr. Gessler," cried the clear, distinct voice of Mr. Beranger. "Were it not for Montaigne, I do believe you would never forgive me."

"It does not require his help," I answered, "to forgive what requires no forgiveness. I have been charmed and interested."

"You must also forgive me, Mr. Gessler, if the questions I am about to ask manifest an indiscreet curiosity; but as every young man enters life with a fixed aim and profession, may I ask what are yours?"

"My profession is that of a tutor, Mr. Beranger," I replied; "and my aim" . . . . I hesitated.

"Is success, of course," he put in. "Everyone knows that. Have you come to London to enter any house in that capacity?"

"When I am so fortunate as to obtain an engagement," was my reply. "I am merely an adventurer, Mr. Beranger."

"Ah! then," cried he, "I am a lucky fellow after all; I have a dreamy scapegrace of a nephew up stairs, Mr. Gessler, who is (or fancies himself) a genius; and who, like every real or fancied genius, worries himself and all around him. The fellow is an artist, and is chained to his easel; he paints perpetually, and will not go into the fields or mingle with society. Now the thought has suggested itself to my mind, that a companion of his own age might prove beneficial to him."

"In every probability he would," said I.

"Will you then be the guardian extraordinary of this future Raphael?" cried Mr. Beranger, with that frankness of manner that never seemed genuine. "You possess all the requisite qualifications: youth, health, vigour and gaiety of mind, liberty, and so on. I do not mean to flatter, Mr. Gessler."

"You have done so already, Mr. Beranger," said I. "I feel excessively obliged, and shall be happy to . . . ."

"Watch the aberrations of an insane artist?" laughed he. "For when Shakspeare gave seething brains to the lunatic, the lover, and the poet, he should have added the artist too. I fear you will not be grateful a month hence, Mr. Gessler."

"My only dread is that I shall not have sufficient influence over him to wean him from his easel," said I. "You spoke of gaiety, and I am not gay; I can teach, but not fascinate. You understand my meaning."

Perfectly, but have no fear," said he. "Baptist had too much genuis to be a Greek scholar in his boyhood. Teach him Greek, and let the Grecian goddesses fascinate him."

It was finally arranged that I should enter Mr. Beranger's house as tutor and companion to his nephew, Mr. Baptist Beranger. The salary he offered was magnificent, and I felt elated at my good fortune.

"Come to-morrow morning at this hour,"

said he, at parting. "I dine out this evening, but to-morrow I will introduce you to Baptist. I trust you will find my house as much of a home, as a bachelor's house can be; for Fortune has not thought me good enough for matrimony, Mr. Gessler. But I will leave your domestic comfort in the hands of my worthy housekeeper, and of my gentleman,—not valet, but gentleman—Mr. Trickem."

He shook me heartily by the hand, and we parted.

Before I left Oxford, the flowers of Miss Eagle Marr and the mysterious Florian, whom I supposed to be her brother's betrothed, had been sent to me, and I thought it advisable to deliver them to my old College friend as soon as possible, that he might receive them before they began to fade. I accordingly drove to the address given me by the Major.

Philip's apartments were in a lonely back street, in which poor gentility appeared to be pathetically written on every door and window. He was not at home when I called, but I entered his little parlour and said I would wait for him. The room was plain, but bore evidence of being occupied by a gentleman and a scholar. I took a glass vase, and filling it with water, placed the flowers in it. I had scarcely done so, when Philip Marr, bearing some books and parchments, came in.

His appearance was calm and gentlemanly; his countenance betokened an amiable disposition and refined intellect. His eyes were large, deep, and dark; the features firm and manly; and the complexion, though rather pale, a clear olive. His voice was a rich, full baritone, flexible and soft. One felt in a moment that he was a man of genius, energy, and perseverance,—a man, in fact, with an ambition and a purpose. I felt at once prepossessed by his appearance; but had he displayed less gravity and reserve, and a smaller amount of the intellectual man's pride, self-respect, there would have been more love in the feeling with which I regarded him. He looked at me for some time, then holding out his hand and smiling, he said—

"You are Gerald Gessler, of the University. I seldom see an Oxonian now. I am truly happy to see you. You are straight from Oxford, I suppose? How are all friends there?"

"Perfectly well," replied I. "Major and Miss Marr were the last almost that I spoke to in the town."

"You are very kind," said he. "Away on vacation, eh?"

"Yes, on the long vacation," sighed I. "*Alma Mater* and I have shaken hands for the last time."

"And you sigh because you are a school-boy no longer; because you are free?" exclaimed he. "Well, perhaps you should; when liberty is exile, isolation, and toil, it is natural to sigh for freedom. Any news from Oxford?"

I drew the vase of flowers near him, and said:

"These were sent you by Miss Eagle and Florian; do not blush, I do not know who Florian is. And my only news is, that this same marvellous Florian loves you yet."

"Eagle's news?" said he, leaning his head on his hand.

"And the Major's also," said I.

He seemed to muse, and the expression of his countenance betokened that his reflections were of a painful nature.

"I thought I brought you good news, Mr. Marr?" said I

"And so you have," cried he, raising his head. "I thank you for performing your mission so well, in faithfully conveying to me the news which my father and sister so earnestly wished me to receive—that Florian, my future wife, loves me."

He paused as if embarrassed, and walked over to the window.

"I understand your meaning, Mr. Marr," said I. "I shall never speak to you on this matter again."

"Then we shall be great strangers indeed, Mr. Gessler," replied he; "and that we must not be to each other; for many things forbid it; we have been undergraduates together, and though it may appear a very unimportant matter to you, you have brought me these flowers."

He threw himself down on a couch beside

the open window, and let the murky air of London blow over his brow. There was so much languor in all his movements, that he seemed to me like one who had lost heart, and I sincerely pitied him. Eagle was wrong; he did not value the flowers much; or only as one who knew nothing of her who sent them as tokens of her affection. They seemed to him meaningless things, that would perfume his chamber for a day, and then perish and be thrown away. For Eagle's sake (and for Florian's), I wished him to think more of them. I accordingly took the vase, and seating myself on a chair beside him, said—

"Let me read your letter for you."

He did not comprehend me, and raised his eyebrows.

"These pretty creatures have a language of their own," said I; "and I am more learned than you, for I can speak to them, and they to me."

"That did not occur to me," cried he, growing interested, "I am a lawyer. Flowers are aimless trifles to me, which I smell and forget; but I have a great sympathy with language and words, for they are definite. Read the letter."

"I shall make a tame Ophelia," said I, as I parted the flowers from each other. "I must begin bitterly: here is wormwood, the emblem of absence, and beside it, honeysuckle, the bonds of love, which, for this is the meaning these flowers convey, stretch the whole distance between Oxford and London; then come the hawthorn of hope, the heath of solitude, the thrift of sympathy, and the jasmine of——"

"Never mind the jasmine," said he; "they have sent me sympathy, that is sufficient; and to a man whose time is divided between law and loneliness—strangers and litigants—sympathy from kind hearts in a distant home is very sweet. Show me the flower."

I gave him a twig.

"It is very small and fragile," said he, examining the tiny blue bells of the thrift; "and evanescent too; to-morrow morning these flowers will probably be dead."

"Perhaps not," exclaimed I; "they live longer than a day."

"But they are sure to perish, Mr. Gessler," said he; "sympathy passes away in time."

"You will soon have a more enduring sympathizer," smiled I. "I believe you will not long be a bachelor."

"No, not very long," replied he, abstractedly; "Are you to reside permanently in London, Mr. Gessler?"

I narrated to him my plans and prospects; when he heard my employer's name, he started.

"Mr. Albert Beranger!" echoed he, "that is one of our clients. He is a Constantinople millionaire; a man of immense wealth; but a heathen, a Mohammedan. He is a strange, peculiar man, with many oriental eccentricities, and a bigoted follower of Mohammed. Beware of the heaven of the unbelievers, Mr. Gessler."

"It matters not to me how often he brings his pagan theology on the carpet," said I. "I read the Koran from beginning to end, in Oxford, and think it (the prophet forgive me) stuff. I have little fear of becoming a proselyte."

"It may be your fate—your *kismet*, as the Mohammedans call it—to become one, for aught you know. I am somewhat of a fatalist."

I smilingly answered, that, of all the creeds I knew, fatalism was the one least attractive to myself.

"Yet, after all," I added, banteringly, "it may doubtless be to some people a kind of moral blanket in which they may wrap themselves up. Deny freewill, and accept fatalism, and one may get rid of many of those awkward twinges of conscience which are the consequences of a life's omissions and commissions. But surely you are not in earnest?"

"Possibly not," said Mr. Marr. "The sentiment of to-day may be merely the result of a murky atmosphere and a passing bilious attack. Yet biliousness is not altogether an evil. Do you think Byron would ever have penned those grand bursts of blended misanthropy and melancholy that witched the world's heart to listen to his wild word-music in tears, if his liver had always been in good order? Do you think Thomas Carlyle,

Chelsea's grim Jeremiah, would ever have written 'Sartor Resartus,' had he never known dyspepsia? May not a man's whole career mainly depend on the state of his stomach? Can we not—humiliating thought though it be—resolve much of our virtue, much of our vice—mere relative terms, my dear sir—into the lack or superfluity of bile? Oh, that terrible liver!—am I not an unromantic materialist?—for how much has it not to answer! Possibly for this very outburst. Well, *revenons à nos moutons;* perhaps, after all, there will be no great harm should you in time get to love that elegant pagan of yours, Mr. Beranger."

He was arranging his law papers on the table when he spoke thus.

"I have all this blue paper to fill with dry words before the clock strikes six," added he. "Copying fatigues one more than composition, as the labour is more manual than mental; and I dare not yawn or doze over my work, for a single word erased, omitted, or even illegible, may lead to a suit in Chancery, and curse I know not how many lives. Did you ever hear of the firm of Messrs. Tamper and Leer, Fleet Street?"

I replied in the negative.

"They are my masters, and your employer's solicitors," he continued, "and you will know them well very shortly, for Mr. Beranger has always a great deal to say to them regarding argosies, and dishonest Turks, and Constantinople monetary affairs."

"As you cannot write and talk," said I, "I had better bid you good-bye for the present."

"To return again soon, I hope," exclaimed he, shaking hands.

While I parted from him I told him Eagle's message about the beloved spaniels.

"Ah! poor little Witch and Wizard," cried he; "how they would leap and bark to see me back in Oxford! Come back on Thursday evening (a leisure time with me), and tell me about your Mohammedan."

This is a book with two heroes. Philip Marr is one of them, and Albert Beranger the other. It was my fate to know them both intimately, and to trace them (and another) step by step on to the tragedy of the end. I loved Philip Marr then, and, despite all that has occured since, I love him still with my whole heart. Whatever we said or did, separate or together, we never ceased to be each other's friend for one moment. The thing that sows the deepest hatred and the longest estrangement sprung up between us; yet we did not hate or become estranged. Beneath the common blow that struck us both down, we became the closer friends, and found each other's sympathy and consolation sweet. We stood unconsciously, but inevitably, in each other's path. We wounded each other in the dark, and it was neither his fault nor mine that we felt and acted as we did. Philip Marr is my friend, and Albert Beranger my enemy. This is a fact that must be known, and whatever they say or do no one must think otherwise. My tale will tell why.

Punctuality being one of my most conspicuous social virtues, I did not keep Mr. Beranger waiting for my appearance next morning. I started when I saw him, there was such a terrible and ghastly change on his countenance. His troubled expression and his ghastly hue indicated that, from some cause unknown to me, he must have passed a night of mental torture. At the moment, I attributed the alteration to ill health. Observing the anxious look with which I regarded him, he at once said,

"Yes, Mr. Gessler, I am ill, very ill; but that is the common fate. We all sicken occasionally, but the last is a sickness unto death; yet men rush to their physicans and their drugs, as if these could render them immortal. This is one of the greatest follies under the sun, forgotten by the wise man. In the meantime we will go to Baptist."

I followed him out of the chamber; on the staircase he remarked,

"The votaries of Art and Literature are always literally as well as morally nearer the clouds than other mortals, and generally expatiate in attics. Baptist's rooms are at the top of the house, and he is usually so absorbed in his solitary meditations that it is very difficult to get him downstairs. Make him more sociable and convivial, Mr.

Gessler, and, if possible, make him understand that, living in such solitude he can know nothing of life, and never be a great painter."

I promised to do my best. Mr. Baptist Beranger's apartments were not in the attic, as Mr. Beranger's words would imply, but in the floor beneath. He pushed open a door, and we found ourselves in a *boná-fide* artist's studio. Easels, palettes, busts, statuettes, lay-figures, antique vases, rich draperies artistically disposed on Elizabethan chairs, mediæval panoplies, pieces of armour, swords, shields and stillettoes, etc., with finished and unfinished pictures, hung up in good or bad light, and some in no light at all. The painter himself was standing at a distant easel under the half-shaded window, looking as if he had not performed a very careful toilette that morning. He was young, about my own age, but the beauty of his face was that of ruins, for the light of hope and the blood of health were both exhausted or dead. The large, orientally-shaped, blackly blue eyes were as blank as the pallid cheeks, which appeared cold and livid, as if the living tide that circled through the veins were exhausted. His lips were pale as those of a statue, and although a smile hovered upon them it was one that indicated a sarcastic or bitter feeling. Had the face shown more youth and brightness, and the limbs and muscles more vigour and power, he would have been singularly handsome; but his customary stoop, and the general air of lassitude, gave him an old and broken appearance, though his countenance was occasionally lighted up by the lurid fire of that restless ambition that burnt incessantly within him. His soft, rich, chestnut hair, the curls of which fell in heavy masses over his brow, was the only thing about him that preserved an appearance of youth.

"If he has genius," thought I, "Pietro Wells is right; it is an 'accursed and miserable gift.' He is not a true nature-loving artist, happy in the exercise of his skill, but an ambitious man. Bonaparte's cancer has half covered his soul already. Such a dull honest fellow as I am is no companion for this wild aspiring nature."

CHAPTER III.

AN ARTIST.—SELIM.—MADAME MUSCAT.—MR. BERANGER'S MYSTERIES.

"I'd much rather have a sound digestion, than Bonaparte's cancer."

Mr. Beranger placed his hand on Baptist's shoulder, with such a marvellous look, in which love, bitterness, and regret seemed combined, that, feeling assured there was mystery in their history, I regarded them with a feeling of curiosity I could not restrain.

"Baptist, I have brought Mr. Gessler," said he.

Baptist looked at me with a bold, imperious stare, and bowed, or rather tossed his head.

"He will be agreeable society, truly," thought I; "but then genius never is."

The artist had not made a pleasant first impression.

"You must meet as friends, not strangers," said Mr. Beranger again.

Baptist gave me a blunt, impulsive shake of the hand, and muttered some words of welcome which I did not hear. Then, turning to his easel, he drew his uncle's attention to a picture that stood on it, evidently disdaining my criticism; for in his eyes I was emphatically the *tutor*, and nothing else. I, however, looked at his painting with interest, at which he appeared pleased; for if even a worm could admire, I believe an ambitious man would be delighted with its admiration.

"What do you think of this, now?" said he, alluding to the picture.

It was the life-size "Head of a Seraph," a poetical conception, well executed, of

"The rapt seraph, that adores and burns,"

for this line of Pope flashed through my mind at the first glance; and the one absorbed expression of worship was powerfully yet delicately brought out. The style was bold and dashing, and the effects of light and shade broad, strong, and telling as Rembrandt's; the colouring was warm, rich, and deeply toned.

"I have seen the living likeness of that face," said Mr. Beranger, thoughtfully. "Not that the circle of my acquaintance embraces the seraphim," he added with a smile; "but I have seen it somewhere."

"What does it matter?" cried Baptist, in a sharp, petulant tone. "Does it tell? Is it a good picture? To Jericho with the likeness!"

"Stay!" said Mr. Beranger. "What do you call this picture? I always like to hear the artist's own name for his works. Do you intend that head for a being, or an ideal? Is it a 'Seraph,' or 'Worship?'"

"For both," cried Baptist, impatiently, "as you may see; but I only thought of worship when I painted it; and you may call it 'Worship,' if you please."

"You should have made your seraph a

man, then," said Mr. Beranger, slowly, in a tone of bitter satire.

"What do you mean?" exclaimed Baptist, quickly.

"I mean this," said Mr. Beranger. "Is there not too much of woman about the countenance? It mars and weakens the idea of a seraph's worship."

"I do not understand your meaning," said Baptist. "Stronger love is associated with woman than man."

Mr. Beranger shrugged his shoulders at this remark.

"Let me define worship for a moment," cried he. "It means religious homage—adoration—reverence; no thought of self, or of any other but the being worshipped, is supposed to enter the seraph's mind. Now, no woman could so love."

"I tell you they can!" cried Baptist, angrily and sternly.

"Pooh! you only know them in pictures," exclaimed Mr. Beranger. "Woman can love fondly and blindly; but not faithfully and unselfishly, like this seraph; these are not characteristics of woman's love."

A passionate flush reddened Baptist's face for a moment, as, with a sneer, the ungallant Mohammedan made this remark.

"Surely," said the artist, with a fixed and penetrating look in Mr. Beranger's face, "Surely there is *one* tie of respect that binds man to woman—it is our *mother's* sex! I paint woman beautiful for that! I think woman pure for that! I will love woman for that! Will you never tell me why you hate woman, even on canvas? They are, surely, good enough to paint!"

Mr. Beranger's face was ashy pale, but a glance at his eyes showed that a fearful passion was blazing within; notwithstanding which, he replied, lightly,—

"Yes; they are good studies for Venuses, Cleopatras, Delilahs, and the like; none better. But leave poor mortals the pleasure of thinking that angels and seraphs are *not* women, and that woman is not woman in any other life or world than this. The more nature the greater art; one touch of nature beautifies your paintings more than splendid dashes and rich tints. There is little nature on that picture, except the hair and the lights and shadows; put pearls in the ears and on the brow, and your devotee will make as natural a coquette as a seraph."

This criticism was harsh and unjust; but amusing, nevertheless. Baptist drew his brush over the canvas, and the lovely face of the seraph was obliterated. I could not restrain a cry of regret. He looked at me with a smile of scorn, and, addressing me for the first time,

"Pooh," said he, "anything but perfection is a daub!"

"Show Mr. Gessler your Gulnare," exclaimed Mr. Beranger.

Gulnare seemed on her way to the dungeon of Conrad; an expression of terror and expectation was painted on her beautiful face with the most delicious tints I ever saw; the pomegranate lips were wide, the black lashes raised, and the jet hair hung loose and long on her snowy cymar. She held a lamp and a large key in her delicate hands; and hair, garments, and flame, all seemed agitated by a gust of wind. The inspiration of the poet who had painted Gulnare with the pen was also the inspiration of the artist who had limned her with the brush. She was lovely, but not one atom of soul passed from a single charm; she would have pleased a sultan or an opium-eater, but not me.

"I do not like that picture," said I, "that face is only beautiful; there is a want—not of expression, but of good expression—in the countenance. You have worked out the Mohammedan idea too rigidly and faithfully—you have painted your Gulnare without a soul,—a great want, which strikes one in a moment."

"Oh! Mr. Gessler, for shame; how can you turn critic on so much beauty?" cried Mr. Beranger. "Would you admire some hideous Roman saint—a Saint Catherine or a Saint Mary, or the portrait of ugly De Staël, for instance—before this picture?"

"A thousand times," said I. "You should have blotted out the Houri and left the Seraph. I sigh for her yet."

Mr. Beranger, with his Turkish predilections, sneered at me politely.

"Bravo!" cried Baptist, "I like no man so well as a true, blunt, honest critic; my pictures have never been criticised until now (for praise is not criticism), and I have had my vilest daubs so lauded that I could fling even my best pictures into the fire. I rather like to have myself and my pictures torn to pieces; it requires some of the bone and sinew of genius to live and paint after it; and I am sure I should do both worse (or rather better) than ever after the conflict."

"Yet fame is only praise, after all," said Mr. Beranger.

"Yes, praise, but not flattery," said Baptist. "I will never believe that I have genius till the whole world tells me."

"Does the shadow of coming glory never fall upon your canvas?" exclaimed Mr. Beranger. "Do you never think or dream that you have genius? How can you paint without it? I could not."

"Who could?" said Baptist, with a burning eye. "Some think that a mere love for art, combined even with carelessness as to the result of our skill and labour, whether it be worth a thousand pounds or a sixpence, enables us to achieve the greatest triumphs; but they are wrong. Genius is made only out of the stern stuff of ambition. Painting, without ambition, is like starting on a race without breath."

"And you would not care to paint if you expected no glory?" interrogated I.

"No," replied he. Mr. Beranger smiled silently.

"I shall never get him from his easel;" thought I. These words made him work impatiently with his brushes, as if he itched to paint again. Mr. Beranger rung the bell, and soon after a person whom I supposed to be his valet, Mr. Trickem, entered. He was tall, had a foreign appearance, and, with much French grace and vivacity in his manner, was the personification of a fine gentleman.

"Trickem," said Mr. Beranger, "you will show Mr. Gessler to his apartments. We shall meet again at dinner." Had Mr. Trickem's feet been the feet of time falling on flowers, he could not have trodden more lightly as he left the studio with me, and in silence conducted me to the room set apart for me. I observed in one of the passages on our way a small boy in eastern habiliments. To this picturesque youth Mr. Trickem beckoned, and, as he approached, the apparent son of the Orient salaamed before us.

"Are you going on any little errand for Madame Muscat, Selim?" inquired Mr. Trickem, in a dulcet manner. Selim made some hieroglyphics with his fingers, which I suppose stood for "No," for Mr. Trickem continued,—

"Well, then, lead Mr. Gessler to his suite. '*Au revoir*, sir, *au revoir!*'" and, with this salutation, Mr. Trickem left me to the guidance of the eastern youth. On reaching my *suite* I found that it consisted only, as far as I could see, of a parlour and inner bed-room; but then Mr. Trickem used such elegant terms.

"Everythink here, sir," said the child of the sun, in the tone of one who was selling the house by auction. "Hot water, sir; wery good books out of number; and a quiet prospect from the back winder; poor Booker liked that." Here he appeared affected.

"And who was Booker?" inquired I.

"Gramercy! sir," said the page, sighing; and burying his face in the folds of his oriental skirts, while he seemed to weep bitterly, "he was the last tutor, sir, and Madame never left him till the day of his death. Some said he died of voluntary starvation, sir, for he never ate nothing. But I knows better, sir; his poison was old stories, sir, served up with the dust and mildew on 'em. It was a kind of death-madness a-growing on him, sir. I'm sure he must have been 'appy when the Gallipot told him he was a-dying, anything to come was better than the clatter. I know he looked bright like when the Doctor said, 'Mr. Booker, send for your relations.' It was like saying to a rich man, 'Send for your Shark, and make your will.' 'No, doctor,' says he, 'they have sent for me; I'll see 'em all afore to-morrow's sun comes, shan't I, doctor? I'll be young again to-morrow, never to get old; I'll live again to-morrow, never to die; the meeting of to-morrow will never have a parting. I don't want to see *that* sun again, doctor; close the curtains till it's down.' And he turned round and shut his eyes. That day a tall genelman comed to the hall door, asking for Booker's room; I knowed he was a Pusey or a Methody, for he ducked afore the white 'ooman in the hall Whatever he did to him I don't know, but next day, afore the sun rose, Booker's coffin was in this 'ere room."

Here the oriental skirt was again raised to the sympathetic eye of Selim.

"But I hope, sir," said the narrator, in conclusion, "that you won't allow that lady to come over you in that 'ere style. Booker was a melancholy man, and could never feel at home except among a lot of books. But you ain't like Booker, sir."

Anxious to have the dismal tale of my predecessor's tragic death terminated, I was about to dismiss Selim, and send him to the hotel for my luggage, when a thought struck me.

"How is it," said I, "that with your name and costume you speak English so—so well?"

This last assertion must be understood in a comparative sense; well for an eastern, I meant.

"Marry come up, sir," cried Selim, who indulged in the obsolete expressions, exclamations, and even oaths of the middle ages, slapping his thigh like a court gentleman of the olden times, "that is 'cause I was born at Coventry and eddicated at Whitechapel; and my name is no more Selim than it was Adam's. I was a-christened Joe, sir, and will stick to that 'ere name through anythink in any other cloes."

I gave him the name of the hotel, and told him to return with my luggage. On his departure I took up a book that lay on the table, and began to read; it was the gloomy and half insane ravings of some old German philosopher. I am not superstitious, nor have I ever been so, but the theories of this mystical dreamer (he was an advocate for supernatural appearances), and the memory of Booker defunct, gave me a small thrill of morbid fear. I threw the book away and started up. My apartments were moderately large; the hangings were of a jaundiced green damask, and the furniture was made in the antique Elizabethan fashion, by a modern artificer. The statuettes might have been sculptured in that workshop where all antiquities are made, Birmingham; but they looked as ancient as if they had been exhumed from Herculaneum. One small figure of Janus, especially, struck me as being a masterpiece of art; the twin faces were so alike and yet so different,—the perfect types of naked malignity and malignity with a mask. They seemed terrible and satirical likenesses of two real faces. While gazing at the fire I fell asleep, and dreamt about them. The distant sound of wheels rumbled continually throughout the night. I rose, went to the window, and gazed out into the street, but except the still and silent rows of houses, there was nothing to look at there. It was literally Blank Street. A door was open at the farther end of the apartment, leading into the bedroom of the suite, which likewise was hung with green draperies, the colour of leaves when they become sear and yellow, and always so reminding me of Autumn and decay, that to this day I shiver at the sight of a green curtain. A small bookcase contained some of Booker's library, torn, scrawled, and dog-eared. I examined them, and found them of one class, German works on metaphysical and mystical philosophy, almost making us believe that we jostled spirits at every turn. While I was reading one of them I heard a noise outside my door, and the following conversation reached me :—

"What do I see!" cried a female voice. "You have disobeyed me, boy. I—I—"

"I won't be a heathen no more, ma'am!" blubbered Selim, "and I won't go for to be called Selim. I was a-hired to wear green cloes and buttons, ma'am, and to answer the door, and go of errands, and to bob respectably to ladies and genelmen, and to be called Joe; and not to look like a clown or a harlequin, and be took for a heathen and a 'Indoo selling of songs, ma'am! I won't, ma'am, blow me if I will!"

"Boy, boy!" cried the lady, "you are impertinent; I'll tell Monsieur."

Selim blubbered again.

"Master is a Christian and a genelman, ma'am," said he, "and wouldn't go for to ask me to wear them things; and you ain't my missis, ma'am. Its agin the law to wear them cloes, and I shan't, ma'am."

"Did you ever wear these clothes before last week?" inquired the lady, mildly.

"I'm blowed if I did, ma'am," returned Selim, indignantly. "I never remembers the time, ma'am, when I wasn't respectable, and looked like other coves in buttons, only in this 'ere house. I—I—"

"Don't weep, boy," said the lady. "I only desire you to wear these clothes for a short time. Oriental friends are coming soon to visit your master, and I intended your costume for a graceful compliment to them; they will not remain long."

"I looked a deuced deal better in the green jacket and the silver buttons," said Selim, persistently, "and them 'ere friends of master's can have no manner of taste; I'm sure I looks a Guy," and Mr. Selim laughed shrilly.

"I know you looked very well in your livery," said the lady, "but the national prejudices of Mons. Beranger's friends must be respected, you know."

"I don't respects 'em ma'am, for one," said

Mr. Selim. "The new genelman which is tutor, asked me to go for his traps to the station; and I didn't want to be stoned out of creation by the small coves on the street, so I puts on my own cloes. That's the end of it, ma'am, and here I am."

"Bring in the portmanteaus, Selim," began the lady.

"Joe, if you please, ma'am," interrupted he.

"Well, Joe, go in with the portmanteaus, and I will follow." She accordingly fluttered in. This was Madame Muscat, the housekeeper, a slender, rosy little woman of sixty, with a small bright face, ever lighted up with such a smile that one almost imagined that she herself and everything around her was a witticism which madame enjoyed very much. Indeed, that comic little smirk put the elements of humour in everything. Altogether she was a good-natured, comical little woman, and grew charmingly familiar with me immediately. She curtsied thrice before she spoke a word, then, darting forward, she held out her two hands to me.

"Delighted to see you, Monsieur," cried she. "Happy to make your acquaintance. Do you find these rooms delightful or detestable? Pray tell me; for if you hate them, I will get all the maids in the house up to put them to rights."

"Pray do not trouble," answered I, "they are very nice."

"I am not content with that word 'nice,'" cried she, "nice is not a nice word, Monsieur; it is cold, and expresses nothing. You do not love your apartments; let me see now what I can do to them?" She set her head to one side and made all her grey ringlets and carnation ribbons flutter; I offered her a chair, which she only occupied two minutes.

"Mon Dieu!" exclaimed she, starting up, "what a hideous ornament; what a grinning, ugly, deceitful piece of dirty marble!" She clutched at Janus on the mantelpiece.

"You must not take that away from me, madame!" cried I. "That statuette interests me; I like to look at it."

"Sacré!" exclaimed she, "it is a fiend; a

scurril, a libel! Did you not observe? It resembles Monsieur Beranger."

"I observe the likeness now," replied I. "I did not do so before. The resemblance is singular, and not very flattering." Madame plumped herself down in a chair, and looked at me.

"Whom does that image represent, Monsieur?" said she.

"Janus," replied I. She nodded her head quickly.

"And who was Janus, Monsieur?" interrogated she.

"A Roman god, and a king of Italy," replied I; "he was very prudent and wise." She nodded again.

"He had two heads and two brains, you know;" said she.

"He had two faces," continued I. She nodded silently, and then started from her seat.

"Anything more to do?" cried she, looking round.

"I was thinking of removing these old books, and putting my own in their place," said I. "Where shall I put them?"

"Sacré, yes; a good idea," cried she, "Selim!"

He hastened forward, and carried Booker's library away.

"I had a predecessor, Madame, I believe," said I.

"Mon Dieu, so you had," answered she. "Poor man, he was melancholy mad, asthmatic and bilious, and sometimes had the rheumatism. A more miserable man never lived. I think death was made expressly for such people; don't you think so, Monsieur?"

This was Booker's true history in a few graphic words.

"We always dine at six," said she. "A late English dinner hour; but you can dine alone before us, if you choose."

I protested against this, for I detest being an eremite, especially at meal time.

I peered into Baptist's studio, but there was no hope for Greek that day; he was so absorbed in painting that it was impossible to turn him from it to any other task. I had, therefore, nothing for it but to examine his paintings and engravings, and to turn over his sketches and models, till I or he grew weary. At last, wiping his brush, he took up a book. I started up with delight.

"Greek at last," cried I. "Bravo!"

He smiled and shook his head, as he gave me the volume.

"My head aches dreadfully, and whirls round like a wheel," said he, lying down on a sofa. "Besides, my eyes feel weak, and it would be refreshing to *hear* something now; read some of that to me."

"It is the 'Giaour,'" said I, "you could not have chosen worse poetry for a headache; it is the most vehement and rousing strain ever written."

"What is there in it to make it so?" inquired he. "There is nothing in it that will rouse me. Go on."

How evident it was from this that Baptist had never loved unhappily, or loved at all. He listened calmly; there was not a word about his passion, ambition, in the whole poem. I felt my heart bursting, and my whole soul went back to Oxford and Miss Ryder. I came to the "Giaour's" confession, and those marvellous words of his, whose power, pathos, and fervour are unequalled, moved me so greatly that I had to paùse.

"Are you tired, or are you a good elocutionist?" inquired Baptist. "That falter and pause are very effective indeed."

I swallowed a glass of water, and continued my reading. That old heart, animated only by ambition, never dreamed that I felt as I read. When the story was done, I closed the book.

"Read the 'Giaour's' ride again," said Baptist.

I did so.

"What a picture that would make," continued he, "the black background, the horse's dark neck stretched across the canvas, and the thin white vampire face staring at you out of the darkness, with bright clear blood in the lips,—a real vampire face! To Jericho with rest! I think I shall never rest; even in bed at night, my mind conceives and paints till I sleep."

He took a canvas and began to sketch the

form of his conception. How rapidly and delicately, with what exquisite anatomical skill, he drew the heads of the man and horse! With a few bold and telling strokes here and there, he depicted the hate burning in the one, and the sweat and foam with which the other in its speed was covered.

"Say farewell to the vampire and his horse for to-day," said I, "and let us have a brisk ride in the park. Don't you think you could paint a ride better after you have had a ride yourself? I'm certain you could. I'll ring for Selim."

"Pray do not order horses," said Baptist. "To mount on a horse's back, with dim eyes and a swimming brain, is rather perilous; I cannot ride to day."

This settled the matter, for one could never ask Baptist to do anything twice. At six I descended to dinner, warned to do so by three distinct knells, as if dinner were doom. Mr. Beranger talked of Oxford—of its colleges, student life, scenery, and society,—lightly and skimmingly, but with no remarkable interest. He led me on at last to speak of the Ryders, the last persons in the world of whom I should have thought of speaking.

"Colonel Ryder is a cousin of mine," said he. "We were students together, and the greatest friends in the world; then he became a soldier, and like every other man whose morals are formed in the army, he became gay; that means betting and gaming, Mr. Gessler. Shall I carve for you again, Madame?"

"You must know him well, then?" inquired I, crimsoning.

"Not very, for some twenty years back," replied he. "We had some foolish boyish quarrel when we left college, which has estranged us for all these years; but I mean to forgive him very soon. You have no sherry, Mr. Gessler. We never chanced to meet since his marriage. He was a handsome fellow—a dashing military blade; and he married a Miss Howard, a fortune and a beauty. How many children has he, Mr. Gessler?"

"Three," replied I. "Two sons and a daughter."

"I shall quite blush to meet him," said Mr.

Beranger. " Here I am still, an old bachelor, without even a dog. Trickem discovered a grey hair this morning, Madame."

" Mon Dieu !" cried Madame, raising up her hands. " That is an impossibility."

" The impossibility, however, occurred," said he. " Trickem wanted me to make that grey hair one of my secrets, and to burn it; but I locked it up in my writing case. Does the Colonel wear well? His great terrors were a wig and the gout; have they come yet?"

" A long time ago," answered I,

" And Ryder is a veteran at last!" cried he. " I remember him the smart young Lieutenant, full of jest, amour, and practical joke, trying to gain as many ladies' hearts as would serve for a regiment; and now, I suppose, if he attempted to play the gallant he would be laughed at. So wags the world. Have you finished that picture, Baptist?"

" How could I?" said Baptist, impatiently, " without the woman's face?"

" Nothing is more common or more cheap than a woman's face," replied Mr. Beranger, with a tone of such calm contemptuous irony, that I almost hated him for the words.

"Hear him!" cried Madame Muscat, in an ecstasy. "Mon Dieu, hear him! I recollect a great artist in Lombardy who painted me, and he gave me ever so many gold Napoleons for the sitting, and he had to pray hard before I would consent. Mon Dieu, hear him! common and cheap!"

"You misunderstand me, dear Madame," said he, "a woman's face is worth any amount of *money*; but Baptist, the miser, wants a face that has no price, that cannot be bought; and such a one I will get him, a good, quiet model too, in an old miniature."

He rose up with that expression of pain on his countenance which I had seen on it once before.

"Let me have it immediately, then," said Baptist. "I could paint it well now; perhaps I shall not be able to do so again; for we do not keep bins and bottles full of inspiration beside us; I wish we could."

"I doubt if the divine afflatus would be worth exchanging for this wine," said Mr. Beranger. "I would not give that last hogshead of port for cart-loads of Castalia and Hippocrene; when I drink it I do not envy genius, for to be slightly elated with it is as rapturous as to be mad with inspiration. Try the experiment, Baptist."

"I have done so," said he, shortly, "and I have found that there is a wide difference between inspiration and drunkenness, as much as between the rat that runs in the gutter and the star that burns above it."

"You have drunk too deeply," laughed Mr. Beranger. "There is a middle course, a shallow depth of wine, and this medium degree resembles inspiration the most. Come, now, Baptist, let me teach you the secret."

"I thank you," said Baptist, curtly; "but you will find me an obstinate pupil, the kind of scholar that does not want to learn. I admire your excellent wine very much, and relish two glasses of it, no more, at dinner."

The words were plain, and the sentiment simple; but they aroused Mr. Beranger's anger; he took up a cigar, looked at Madame

Muscat, and then flung it into the fire. Madame hastily seized her fan, gloves, and handkerchief, and rose from her chair.

"Pray, Monsieur," said she, "begin your dear smoking; I must attend to my tarts and *entrées*, you know. Do tell me, gentlemen, before I go, what you thought of the fish sauce, it was an original recipe—too pungent, perhaps, you think."

"Not at all, Madame,—not in the least," said Mr. Beranger, "it was exquisite—exquisite—like its inventor."

Madame curtsied, shook her fan, her ribbons and her ringlets, and glided out, casting a peculiar look on me as she went.

Mr. Beranger extracted two cigars from his case, and offered one to me, which I took, but with no intention of smoking it.

"I am afraid to offer one to you, Baptist," said he, smiling bitterly, "lest you might think it another attempt to demoralize."

"I choose to be moral," said Baptist, sternly; "and I therefore do not choose to smoke your cigars or pipes again."

Each word was spoken emphatically, and

Mr. Beranger coloured, why I did not then understand, but I do now.

"What a wonderful casuistry is yours," said Mr. Beranger; "there is sin in whiffing a few puffs of smoke."

"Out of some pipes," said Baptist, moving to the door.

Mr. Beranger sat perfectly silent, veiling his face with smoke; and I sat at the table, playing with some filberts and a nut-cracker, for some time after he left; then he threw away the fag end of a cigar, and went out also, and I saw him no more that night.

When I next saw Baptist, he was painting a strange picture—a dark graceful maiden stood facing us on the canvas, her beautiful countenance lighted up by intellect; she might have been kneeling, praying to be delivered from the agony depicted in her face. But she was very haughty and erect, although the expression of her countenance indicated that her feelings were too deep for utterance. Three youths were standing opposite to her in academic costume, two erect, the third with his head buried in his arms, as if overpowered by some great emotion. It was one of the "tricks of the trade" to hide away the three faces from us; for one felt a burning curiosity to know something about the prayer—the passions it appealed to or awoke, and the answer it received.

Mr. Beranger took a deep interest in this picture; for hours he would watch Baptist painting it, and seemed more like a teacher than a spectator, for he pointed out certain faults, and dictated certain directions, which Baptist blindly followed. The face of the lady struck me; it was the perfect likeness of Kilda Castellon, or, rather, of Madame Castellon when she was Kilda's age. What struck me even more was that the face was copied from a miniature in Mr. Beranger's possession.

Mr. Beranger was a man of peculiar, or at least characteristic habits; after dinner he would sip a glass or two of wine, and, merely for my encouragement, smoke a cigar. Then he would retire to a small private room in the attic, the interior of which no one had ever seen, and locking himself in, would remain there for some hours, and sometimes for the whole evening. When he came out, he generally looked wasted, wan, and exhausted, like an ascetic monk coming out of a penance cell in Lent. But the truth was, that in Mr. Beranger's constitution, as in that of most Asiatics, the sensual predominated over the intellectual; and no one would ever dream of his being either a scholar or a devotee. It was plain, then, that the small, unseen chamber was neither a study nor an oratory. He was also in the constant habit of taking short and secret journeys from home; sometimes returning with thoughtful brow, in a dark gloomy mood; and at others with excited spirits, hope gleaming in his eyes. Curiosity is one of our strongest passions, and these mysterious customs of his fretted it keenly. Besides he was one who managed to create an interest even with regard to his most trivial habits. I used to watch him with intense attention when carving, mixing up his mulled wine, or rolling a cigarette.

The old farmer, delighting in long clay pipes and home-brewed barleycorn, whose daughter averred that whenever she wished to ask him a favour she always chose "pipe-time of a night," for then he was best tempered, never knew one half the dreamy delight experienced in the consumption of the fragrant weed by Mr. Beranger. Only to see him rolling up a cigarette delicately, as though he loved it—to see him in languid luxury puffing spiral clouds of blue smoke through his parted lips, while in a low musical voice he descanted on subjects most interesting to me, with an eloquence all his own,—would have been in itself a stronger argument in favour of tobacco's benign influence, than any men who, unable to smoke themselves, rail at smoking and smokers alike, could bring against a custom which, to say the least, has the merit of preserving the mind of an idle man from total vacuity, while lulling his world-worn brain.

I was sitting with him when he was in the state described, when, after a pause of some minutes in our conversation, he asked—

"Did you ever read 'Shelley,' Mr. Gessler? Did you ever read 'Shelley?'"

"Oh! yes, a thousand times; he is my favourite poet,—his poetry is clear and pure, his beautiful verses sounding like the richest music."

"Do you like his poetry?" said he. "I do not, for his infidelity seemed to be his inspiration, and I do not like a man that has not some god or other; let him pray, if it were only to the African's wisp of grass and straw. But I must remember to tell you about the Elysium. Do you recollect that line in Shelley, 'Common as light is love!' The thought is true and sweet. Elysiums are common as love therefore, Mr. Gessler, for they go together."

"I know it," said I. "I mean I believe it."

"I know it and believe it;" said he, growing warm and excited. "And I am a happy man, for I can reach my Elysium any time, by train, in a few hours."

"Ah! this explains your mysterious journeys," said I.

"You are right," replied he; letting the smoke cover his face. One cause of curiosity was elucidated; he was a suitor.

"You will soon cease to be a bachelor, then?" said I.

"That depends upon one word, nothing more," replied he, smiling. "Upon that word, which stands between every living man and matrimony—'yes' or 'no.'"

"I sincerely trust you may have a 'yes,' Mr. Beranger." I saw that his feelings were deeply engaged, and I said this fervently.

"I thank you, Mr. Gessler," he said, "but you hint at the terrible possibility of a 'no.'"

"It is easily said, Mr. Beranger," replied I. "It is often said; it is spoken to thousands of us; you and I may be of the number."

Strange to say that with all his love, and experience of men and the world, this possibility—a very probable one, I thought—never seemed to have struck him before. I saw that if a rejection came he would not be prepared for it. How fierce are men's passions and desires! They smoulder as age comes on, but even their whitest ashes are warm. He rose up quickly, as though some passing thought had stung him.

"I should have been your age, Mr. Gessler," said he, "and you mine, for you have so much reason and I so little. I have left vanity far behind me, but I love so deeply that the very suggestion of failure pricks me like a needle."

He soon after went to his secret chamber, and the following day departed on his journey. After a week's absence he returned, but looking so pallid and miserable that I feared the word "no," had separated him and his beloved for ever. He went more frequently than before into his small chamber, and remained there longer than usual, looking paler than ever when he came out.

I had been a resident in London for a considerable time, during which I experienced the warmest and most uniform kindness from Madame Muscat and Mr. Beranger; but during a period of many months I had not once performed the duty of a tutor. My position was therefore exceedingly irksome, as it entailed upon me the heavy labour of idleness, combined with the disagreeable conviction that I was handsomely paid for doing nothing. I did indeed read to Baptist the rousing poetry and prose he liked; and I spoke to him when he desired conversation; or spread out his colours on a palette, and sometimes sat for certain models; but all this was teaching neither Greek nor anything else. I often urged him and Mr. Beranger to allow me to begin my duties. The former would merely shrug his shoulders, and the reply of the latter invariably was,

"Till he finishes this picture, which he paints for me, Baptist cannot compose his mind for study; for art, after woman, is the most jealous and tyrannical mistress in the world; therefore, Mr. Gessler, it would be doing your powers injustice, to give you a pupil with half his mind at his easel. But a very few days will now complete it, and then the longer you keep him from canvass and paint the better."

I had to put time to the best and most agreeable uses possible under these circumstances. I became what I never expected to be, a good correspondent, and wrote letters which I never intended to have written. For in this enforced leisure I flew to correspondence as an agreeable employment. I made frequent visits to Philip Marr; and did not regret my monotonous idleness, since it cemented our mutual love, and made us fast friends.

CHAPTER IV.

MR. BERANGER'S VISITORS.—MADAME CASTELLON.—PHILIP.—TWO LAWYERS.

"Whate'er he be, 'twas not what he had been."—*Byron.*

ONE day Selim burst into my room, with his muslin turban in one hand, and a valise in the other.

"They're comed, sir," said he, "the dark friend of Mr. Beranger; and marry come up, sir, if he don't look like a Turk? There's his name, sir; I ain't good at reading writing, sir, please, sir."

I read for his edification the name on the valise,—"Dr. Mustapha, from Constantinople to London."

"He is a Turk, you see," said I, "for he comes from a city in Turkey, and has a Turkish name."

"I thought he comed from a worst place," said Selim, donning his turban, "for he ain't at all good to look at, sir; he stood in the hall silent like, sir, and his eyes glared on me like two lamp-posts; then he said something to me, Master knows what, and pointed to the valise. I took it, and bolted. I wish to goodness he had stopped in Constantinople!"

Selim sat down on the valise to ejaculate this prayer.

"Why do you detest this foreign doctor?" said I.

"I don't hate him, sir," replied he, "I only don't like to look at him, 'tickler so be as it was night, or to be alone with him; the feelings that we 'ave to churchyards, sir."

From that moment the Doctor became one of Selim's antipathies, and, as was his wont, he invested him with supernatural qualities; for he "scorned the doctrine of the Sadducee,' and believed as firmly in spirits as in bricks and mortar.

I met Dr. Mustapha and Mr. Beranger that evening. The former had a loose Turkish dress, short, and with few folds, as if the picturesque had been sacrificed for the comfortable. He also wore a crimson cloth fez, with a black silk tassel. I had but a brief glance, for Mr. Beranger merely introduced us, and then walked on; and despite all Selim's dark hyperbole, I felt no deeper emotions in Dr. Mustapha's presence than I would have experienced in that of any other unknown foreign gentleman in undress. His complexion was dusky, and his hair and beard were coal black; but he was not by any means repulsive or ill-looking. There was, at times, a furtive expression of wit and humour on his fat olive countenance, which he could mask under an aspect of the most solemn gravity. He was a gossip, and luxurious, or rather lazy; loving, while he held forth, to sit native fashion on a sofa, with cushions on every side, a hookah in his mouth, and comfits on a plate near him. He spoke tolerable English, but could be very obscure and idiomatic when he chose.

Mr. Beranger's other visitor may be as

great a surprise to my readers as she proved to myself.

A few days after the advent of the dark doctor, I went into a small sitting-room, and fell upon a strange lady, who sat at a window sewing. She turned her head as I entered, and I found, to my wonder, that she was Madame Castellon, from Oxford.

"Madame Castellon!" ejaculated I, holding out my hand.

"Madame *Mellitton*, at your service," said she, curtseying.

"I am surprised and delighted to see you in London," said I. "I trust you are all well."

"*I* am well, sir," replied she, stiffly.

"And Miss Castellon and the Doctor," inquired I.

"While I remain in London they are nothing to me, sir," said she. "In this house I am neither the wife of the one nor the mother of the other, so pray do not trouble yourself to inquire for them, or to call me by their name. This is my apartment, sir; can I do anything for you?"

"Do I intrude, Madame?" said I.

She lifted her dark eyes.

"Perhaps you do," said she, "if you have as little to say to me as I have to say to you at present."

"You speak as if we had never met until this moment," replied I. "I am not aware of having given you any cause for this coldness, and regret if I have unconsciously done anything to offend."

I paused, and the shining bodkin rose and fell in the sunbeam: then she laid down the cambric web.

"Do you think you could offend me?" interrogated she; "or make me colder than I am—than I have been made?"

"It is possible, madam!" replied I.

"It is *not* possible!" said she. "Do not think you have any part or parcel in my coldness. I have some work to do (I am doing it now); when it is done I will not be so cold. I have more interest in you than you dream of; a thought of you mixes with my most important thoughts. Do not look surprised. Pray draw down the curtain, the sun blinds me."

"Am I to address you as Madame Mellitton?" said I, "and speak to you as my old friend Madame Castellon?"

"I spoke to you before on that subject," replied she. "You never knew a Madame Mellitton before, did you?"

"No; I never did," said I.

"Then you must not know me as Madame Mellitton either. You asked for Kilda; she is very well, but she must not hear from you that I am here. You must treat me entirely as a stranger, and neither converse nor write about me."

"Must I also deceive Mr. Beranger?" inquired I.

"You will not deceive," cried she, sharply; "am I not a stranger to you? What do you know of me?"

I felt considerable curiosity till dinner-time. It was gratified then, however, for both the visitors sat down to dinner. Dr. Mustapha was now attired in vesture of familiar cut, and looked very *distingué* in English full dress. He was emphatically "Doctor," or his looks belied—(I beg the faculty's pardon)—I mean flattered him very much. Madame Mellitton (so I shall call her) was plainly dressed, yet as I thought, in good taste. She wore a black crape gown fastened at the neck and wrists, yet transparent on the bosom and arms. Strings of coral beads were round her throat, coral earrings in her ears, and coral bracelets on her arms. A small black velvet cap concealed the whole of her glittering jet hair, except a brace of heavy curls which hung at each side of her head, a dark background to the small ears, and relieving the scarlet pendants suspended from them. The attire was plain and unadorned, yet it could not take away the rich Eastern aspect, which showed that she came from adistant sunny clime.

As I went down to dinner I passed the sitting-room where I had first seen her. The door stood partially open, and voices sounded from within;—they were those of Madame Mellitton and Mr. Beranger. The lady's words were partly those of prayer, and partly of menace. But the bland satire—the urbane scorn—with which Mr. Beranger met her petition, showed that he was unmoved by it.

I felt it was vain for Madame to press her suit longer. I did not understand a word of the language in which they spoke, but a name here and there—that of Pietro Wells, Baptist, and my own—excited my curiosity. Why did Madame Castellon or Mellitton, utter my name so earnestly; sometimes with anger, and sometimes apparently in the language of prayer? What was Hecuba to me, or I to Hecuba?

After Madame Mellitton's entrance into the room, I observed that Baptist, during some light conversation on the topics of the day, frequently gazed curiously towards her, and, after a short time, turning round, entered into conversation with her.

"Have we ever met before, Madame?" said he.

"Perhaps we have," answered she, as she bent over her plate, with her bright eyes glittering at Mr. Beranger from under her black lashes.

He looked at her again, and his face flushed.

"Perhaps we have not met; I may only

have seen you before," said Baptist. "My recollection is very faint, as if that of a dream."

Mr. Beranger looked ill at ease; and Dr. Mustapha changed the conversation by telling some remarkable story of a dream he had once heard. But Baptist had something on his mind.

"May I request the favour of your portrait for a painting, Madame Mellitton?" said he, suddenly.

"Some faces cheat the portrait painter," answered she, quietly, "and mine is one of them; you will never be able to paint *me*. The thing that is truly us, never leaves us, or goes out of us, or is seen apart from us. Do you know this?"

"Yes; I have not only known it but mourned it," said he. "But I wish you to represent some one; the character, however, may not flatter you."

"No character that you could paint would," said she. "Make it a natural likeness if you can, but do not flatter. When I was twenty I had my miniature painted; Mr. Beranger, will you return me the——"

"The ketchup?" interrupted he, quickly. Certainly, madame."

"Nature is the painter's art, Madame Mellitton," said Baptist; "to copy natural objects faithfully is more wonderful than to create imaginative objects beautifully."

"I have no doubt of it, Mr. Baptist," said she. "If I could learn the art of painting without the labour of study, I should make a great artist, for I have the faculty; I love colour—a soft tint delights my eye more than music delights my ear. I stood for several wild pictures when I was younger; would you like me to describe them?"

"Yes," said Baptist, "and I will then see if you have the artist's faculty."

"I confess, I think I have," replied she. "I will take more of that *entrée*, Mr. Gessler. In one picture I was represented as a dark dethroned queen, sitting scowling on her rebellious subjects, with her broken crown beside her; I remember the cruel artist tore the fine velvet robe into shreds, and battered the rich jewels. In another I was a poor half-naked slave, rushing through tangled shrubs and branches (amid which horrid reptiles crawled and glistened), with broken and bloody chains hanging to my feet. Do you know, I shuddered to see myself dropping with blood, and my poor hands torn and gashed with the briars. Then he represented me as a crouching woman (a veil, beneath which a knife glittered, thrown over me), kneeling and praying to a man for some great boon which he would not grant." She paused, and Mr. Beranger slowly glanced at her from under his heavy eyelids.

"Did you ever hear the narrative of that picture?" said he.

"No," replied she, "the artist never told me, but I fear he made me something dreadful."

The two pair of dark eyes met each other like lances.

"Something that people hang," said he, "a murderess?"

"Oh! not quite so bad as that, Mr. Beranger," cried she; "perhaps a robber."

"Strange what orators you painters are," said Mr. Beranger, turning to Baptist; what a marvellous eloquence in expression! I remember a picture——"

He paused, to help himself to the leg of a turkey. His carving was always a long and silent operation; and it stopped his story. Madame Mellitton sat quivering on her chair during the process; her lips grew white as her teeth, and shook like the lightest ringlet that hung behind her ear. She did not look nervous or hysterical, nor do I think that she was constitutionally either; yet simple words and looks of Mr. Beranger's have made her tremble and change colour like a child in the dark. Then Mr. Beranger lifted his eyes, and spoke:—

"Will you have a heart, Madame Mellitton? Do not say 'no;' it is not mine, but the turkey's, the softest of the two, probably!" He smiled. "You will not! It is well for me that I did not rashly change places with the turkey in the hope of a 'yes.'"

"I thank you, Mr. Beranger," said she, stiffly. "I will have none." Her voice was hard and dry, as she added, "But you have forgotten the picture you were talking about just now."

"Ah! so I have," cried he. "It is a pity."

Madame Mellitton looked disappointed. Mr. Beranger was evidently playing with her fears.

He suddenly leaned his head on his hand and groaned.

"There is that terrible spasm come again, Mustapha," said he, thickly and hoarsely. "It is dreadful to have a painful and nameless illness like this."

"I told you what would do you good," said Dr. Mustapha. "Travel—change of air and place; leave this great gulf of fog and clamour, London, and break your meerchaums. Bismillah! you will be well enough then."

Whither could I go where I have not been?" said Mr. Beranger. "Were I to seek any country, I should only be going back to old familiar things, which I had used up and exhausted already. I have been everywhere, and the rapture of travel is no more for me. I had better remain in London."

"If you do," said Dr. Mustapha, "you will soon have to travel to a place where, I warrant me, you have never been before. But a man's will is stronger than a thousand dromedaries, and carries him to ruin faster. The prophet knows how I feel the sin against him; but I'll take another glassful out of that red bottle, Beranger."

Although Dr. Mustapha was a Mussulman, yet he consumed as much wine as any thirsty Christian. But even wine itself could not move his stoic philosophy, or shall I say Turkish phlegm? He sat calmly sipping his claret, casting a keen satirical glance at Madame Mellitton, while Mr. Beranger leaned his brow upon his hand and groaned. I offered the latter a glass of water, which he took and partially drank; after a while he rose from his chair and pronounced himself to be better.

"Bismillah! are you?" said Dr. Mustapha, chewing a comfit. "I am surprised to hear it."

During her residence in the house, Madame Mallitton managed to gain a wonderful influence over Baptist. When she did not visit him in his studio, he would seek her in her own apartment, where he would spend hours in her society. What he saw in her to fascinate him so I could not imagine, as, in my opinion, she was not a person calculated to charm and attract; being austere, reserved, uncommunicative, and sometimes cynical and caustic. Baptist did not exact from me now even the small light services which I have before mentioned. I therefore spent almost every evening with Philip Marr. On one occasion I found him in an unusual mood—excited, uneasy, and preoccupied, beginning several subjects of conversation, and then abruptly dropping them.

I asked him if he were ill?

"Perhaps I am," said he, "for my mind is ill at ease. I had a letter from Florian to-day. She is troubled, and will not tell me her troubles. She will be married very shortly, and Heaven knows with what rapture I look forward to our union. And yet, Gessler, she writes about the future despondingly."

"It is strange, to say the least of it," said I.

"It is more," cried he, vehemently, "it is cold, selfish, unloving. I have given her a heart which never knew a thought of love till I saw her. She ought to love me, for I am devoted to her, and when she is my wife she *must!*"

"I feel certain she loves you as much as your heart could desire," said I. "Hers may be one of those timid and retiring natures which do not show half their love till after marriage. To be coy is one of woman's arts."

"She cannot understand my passion," he cried. "I sometimes wish that I had loved a woman more demonstrative, more passionate—a very shrew like Katherine; for I can never regard love as a mere numb and passive feeling."

"You can see faults in your divinity," said I, smiling.

"Not faults in her," cried he, "she is perfection, but in her love for me. Like Othello, I have garnered up my heart with her, and she returns me nothing but letters like these!" throwing me a small white note.

"DEAREST PHILIP,—Are you very sad

and dispirited? Eagle thinks you are, but I do not perceive it in your letters; to think this will make us all very sorrowful. Pray satisfy us on this point in your next letter. You study too much, I fear, to be anything but morbid and gloomy. Try and get down to see us soon. This is my favourite month—delightful June,—and you never saw our roses so beautiful as they are this year; I send you some of their leaves, but I fear their perfume is pressed out.

"Oh! joyful news, poor dear Marrie is better, and is able to walk out with me. I had a letter from darling Frank to-day; his regiment will soon be stationed in London. Papa and the Major are quite vigorous, card-playing as usual. You are angry because I cannot see any sunshine in the future; I shall not write of it again, but will only say that I will do all I can to make it bright for you. We can all exist and bless others without being happy; dear Philip, I will live for you, believe me. I cannot write more, Mark is calling me from the next room.—I am, your own loving FLORIAN."

I paused.

"And you see no love in this letter?" said I.

"Yes, some," replied he, "but it is both scant and cold."

"You are difficult to be satisfied," exclaimed I, sighing. "Did I receive such an epistle from a certain lady, it would be unspeakable delight to me."

"Read the last few lines again," said he; "fancy the writer of it the worship of your soul, and tell me is there nothing there that you would cavil at?"

"Yes," said I, after reading it over again, "she finishes her letter too suddenly; but she explains to you the reason of this."

"Psha!" cried he, impatiently; "it is not that; these lines tell plainly enough that all the love between us is my love. Her coldness makes me miserable. You say you love; tell me the story."

To tell this story of my passion for Miss Ryder was rapture to me; I told him the whole tale minutely, suppressing the name. Mr. Marr listened with attention, and when I ceased speaking, said,—

"Your story is so unlike every other lover's story that it interests me; I hope its termination will be a happy one."

"Do you think there is any hope of that?" said I, shaking my head. "I may have a rival, although I know it not."

"We all have rivals," said he. "If our mistress is beautiful, her own beauty is the lover's rival; if she is domestic, her home; if studious, her books; if gay, her freedom. Only in very rare cases do we ever gain a whole heart."

"Yet every lover thinks his own one of these rare cases," said I; "and though you may laugh at me, I confess I think my own an exception to your dreary rule."

"Happy for you if you do," cried he. "I either want too much, or I lack faith and confidence, and hence my misery."

"You are a strange anomaly," said I; "you ought to be confiding and trusting, and yet you doubt Florian's love, the assurance of which, if I were you, I would not exchange for any of the gifts of genius."

"Let me explain," said he, "why I am sceptical of love. Do you remember Arthur

Bickerstaff in the University? He was cold, reserved, repulsive; no one loved him; he was shunned; and what is he now? One of the greatest and best men in the Church. Then there was that handsome scapegrace, Sherry, who almost every day committed some disgraceful act; how he was caressed and adored! I wish I were not such a great observer of humanity, for it cannot stand too close a test. How does Sherry progress now?"

"He's the same old rascal," said I, laughing. "I remember how dreadfully frightened I was lest he should find out my love, and lay siege to her heart. For the first time I will be inquisitive, Marr, and ask you the other name of your betrothed."

"I was just going to ask you that question," said Philip.

At this moment a gentleman was announced, and the conversation was interrupted.

How often, unknown to themselves or others, a man's life, fate, destiny, and doom may hang on a word or a look. It was so in this instance.

I was in the library one afternoon, mounted

on the summit of a ladder, searching for a book on the top shelf, when two gentlemen entered, both having that appearance of easy-going rate-and-tax paying respectability which good black broad-cloth bestows on the worst of us.

"Can we wait for Beranger?" said one of them, pulling out his watch. "I promised to see Jeffreys at Temple Bar in the course of the evening. The man has never ceased perspiring with haste since his case began, and evidently thinks that law will hurry itself for him."

The other shook his head and said softly, "He ought to find out his mistake. We must see our client to-night, although Jeffreys should dissolve on the street."

With this amiable remark he took his friend's arm.

"Did you see that promising case for Doctors' Commons last night, eh, Leer?" said the other, with a nudge and a chuckle, by no means delightful to see or to hear.

"I confess," said Mr. Leer, putting on his glasses, "that I did not. I never search for cases that show the ulcers of our social system. But who were those sinners, Tamper?"

"You come it this way over the world, Leer," replied Mr. Tamper, with a wonderful ring of sincerity in his laugh; "and are thought to be (by courtesy) a pious man. Oh! Leer, Leer."

"But this is business," continued Mr. Tamper, gravely; "fees before ethics, and costs before doctrines, by all means. But is it possible that you did not see it?"

"No," returned Mr. Leer, with a snivel of emotion. "You look out for divorce, and I for death. My client, I sorrow to say—is—is dying."

"Why, why, Leer," ejaculated Mr. Tamper, looking astounded, "you are getting blunt,—blunt as honesty itself. I'll not insult a man of your intellect by saying that you are honest. But take care, Leer, candour is next door to it. But Mr. Beranger is not so sepulchral-looking as all that," continued Mr. Tamper. "You have a particular affection for the wills; now I, as a person of a more volatile disposition, like the bills better, eh? And I have the best chance this time. Sir J. has a habit of thinking himself in love; now you and I, Leer, don't believe in love any more than in hydras; and that confounded love (don't start) makes more knaves and fools than anything else in the world. Lady J. is a woman, and that is a sufficient guarantee for *her* folly."

"But I would suggest——" began Mr. Leer.

"Don't," said Mr. Tamper, "don't! Since we were boyish lawyers of forty (and you made *that* suggestion) your advices have generally been very good, but supererogatory; they would hang men over again, that like good felons had hung their time. Don't, it is time for you to be practical."

Mr. Leer seemed to revive an old disused custom of his, for he blushed and looked shy.

"Why do you hunt up that old legend?" said he, ingenuously. "A mere youthful indiscretion, too! And you recollect, that I would not oppose you in that case, Tamper."

"As you have so good a memory, perhaps you also remember that you would not be retained for counsel," said that warm-hearted gentleman, Mr. Tamper, playfully.

"Beware, my dear Tamper," replied the Christian Leer, "of a process of law called an action for libel."

"Pooh!" said the blunt Tamper. "Your friend and client put that in his dying confession, before he died in the Gazette, and was buried in the workhouse."

"We will let these old memories rest," said Mr. Leer. "Mr. Beranger is to make his will to-night, and you will be surprised to hear that the heir is his cousin . . . ."

CHAPTER V.

THE DARK PHYSICIAN GETS A PATIENT.—MR. LEER AND A WILL.—MR. BERANGER'S LONGEST JOURNEY.

> "To go we know not where."
>
> *Shakspeare.*

The name was spoken in a whisper.

"You tell me this little item of legal gossip, my dear Leery," said Tamper, "just because you know that I knew it before; it is a way of yours. I wish the man would come, it is getting late."

"I am pained, Tamper, to see that you suspect even me, and are *always* a lawyer; now one should not always feel the lawyer, it is sinful."

"That remark," said Mr. Tamper, with

that significance of eye for which I afterwards heard he was remarkable, "is candour again —and supererogation; but I wonder that a clever devil like Beranger should leave his fortune to an old military spendthrift like his cousin; he lives in Cambridge, does he not? Marr knows him, I think."

"Marr conducted that case for us with a great deal of ability," said Mr. Leer. "I admire his principles."

"He could get through a brief as well without them," said Mr. Tamper; "but Marr makes a capital lawyer. He will shine at the bar some ten years after this, when he is tired of being a plodding solicitor, and has 'gone in' for the bar instead. There's another hour."

Then they went to a distant window; the idea that I had been a willing and dishonourable eavesdropper now presented itself to my mind. I leaped down from my altitude, and laid my hand on Mr. Tamper's arm. Perhaps it was a morbid predilection, but I liked him better than his amiable friend, who put on his glasses and looked at me.

"Sir," said I, "will you permit me to say a few words to you? Perhaps I ought to have spoken earlier."

"Confession never comes too late," said Mr. Leer, speaking to me as if I were a penitent malefactor. "Keep nothing back; speak out."

"I was taking down a book," said I, "and I overheard all your conversation."

"Hem!" exclaimed Mr. Leer, removing his glasses, and looking disappointed, "I believe we did not criminate or commit ourselves in anything, Mr. Tamper?"

"Will you never remember that little saying about the weasels never being found asleep?" replied Mr. Tamper. "We are too old for new habits now. Will you favour me with your name, sir?"—I did so.—"Well, Mr. Gessler, let me be candid, as I very frequently am, and ask you a question. How long were you up on that ladder?"

"Since you came into the room," said I. "Then the thought struck me that I had been eavesdropping, and——"

"After we were too far away for you to

hear our conversation," interrupted Mr. Tamper, "you were seized with a fit of conscience. Do you know, I think your casuistry peculiar, Mr. Gessler, but I find no fault with it."

I blushed crimson at this sarcastic doubt of my honour, which in one sense was deserved. Mr. Beranger entered, and seemed considerably amazed at the group before him; I hastened to explain my dilemma, and he smiled.

"Did you gather many secrets?" said he, "or become acquainted with some professional conspiracy or other? Have I kept you waiting, gentlemen?"

Mr. Tamper, to my surprise, wished an exchange of cards. This proceeding seemed to excite Mr. Beranger's wonder also. As for Mr. Leer, he did not appear to be susceptible of the emotion of surprise.

Baptist did not join us at dinner that day. He had been inspired by some conception suggested by Moore's "Loves of the Angels," and remained at his easel.

Mr. Beranger was also absent, closeted with the lawyers. There was little conversation at the dinner table, for Madame Mellitton was abstracted and silent, while Mustapha, the pagan epicurean, was wholly engrossed by a favourite dish. He was never voluble in this lady's presence; but later in the evening, when Mr. Beranger and I were seated in the smoking-room, he became more eloquent.

"Bismillah! Mr. Beranger, do you know that boy Selim is very observant. I believe he watches all our looks and actions, and listens to all we say."

"You can easily elude Selim's ears," said I. "Speak Turkish."

Dr. Mustapha's eyes twinkled as he said,—"We cannot put our acts in Turkish, Mr. Gessler."

"Even if your acts are watched, Mustapha," said Mr. Beranger, "what need you care? The other side of a locked door is safety enough from all prying and intrusion. You have the *entrée* of my little room upstairs; go in there and keep your doors locked."

"Have you seen Baptist's portrait of me?" said Dr. Mustapha, passing suddenly to another subject. "I sit in his canvas an old sultan, with a pretty slave at my feet, a young

Nourmahal, with coal black hair—and he has done with me. I can do anything for him now. Then Madame Mellitton——"

Just then Selim entered and took away a book; but Dr. Mustapha was too quick for him.

"What have you there, Selim?" cried he.

"A book, sir," and Selim looked sullen and moody.

"So I see! I have eyes. Who is it for?"

"For Madame Mellitton, sir."

"What is its name?"

"Don't know, sir."

Dr. Mustapha motioned to me with dignity. I took the book from the boy's hand, and read the name aloud.

"It is 'Bradshaw's Guide,'" said I.

"I admire Madame's literary taste," said Dr. Mustapha, "nothing but pure facts; but there is obscurity, I admit there is obscurity."

"Take the book away, and begone," said Mr. Beranger, "and in future, if Madame Mellitton wants books, go to the library for them."

"Did I not tell you?" said Mustapha, when

Selim was gone. "The eavesdropper always pops in at the important name; what was I saying when he entered, oh! I was talking about Madame Mellitton. Have you a country house, Beranger? All English gentlemen have their—what do they call them?—suburban villas."

"Would you like a little pastoral pleasure in the green fields?" said Mr. Beranger.

"Pooh! I'll wait till I get to the banks of the Bosphorus," said Dr. Mustapha. "Mr. Gessler, will you excuse a little Turkish? Do not think that I enjoy speaking Turkish; no, talking English is always a relief and a pleasure to me, novelty invariably is; but there are some sentiments which I can only express in Turkish."

He then began to speak in that sonorous language, amid great puffs of smoke. Mr. Beranger merely replied with short 'hems!' and nods; he was too polite to appear interested in what I could not understand.

"Now I'm done!" cried Dr. Mustapha, with a sigh of relief. "English for the next week. Won't you smoke, Mr. Gessler? Well, you enjoy the most delicious part of smoking, the fragrance. Do your boots creak ?—pardon the question, but English boots always creak, Turkish slippers never. Yours do not? If so, please open the door."

I did so, and saw Madame Mellitton standing without, her eyes and teeth shining in a dark corner. I came quickly away. Dr. Mustapha eyed me keenly through a puff of smoke, and then looked at Mr. Beranger and smiled.

"Does Mr. Baptist always paint?" said he.

"Constantly," answered I, "from dawn till darkness."

"An injurious practice," said he. "Where does he get his lovely female models?"

"I do not know," said I; "they were all painted before I came here."

"That picture where I am the sultan is a recent work; who is Nourmahal?" exclaimed he.

"Her face is hidden," said I. "It required no model, she sits with her back to us, but I believe Madame Mellitton sat for the figure."

Mustapha shook his tassels and cried,

"One lovely arm is flung over my knee; the attitude is graceful and affectionate, and I sit like a royal worshipper of beauty looking down into her upturned face; pity that the fairest countenance is hidden. Madame Mellitton is Nourmahal, Beranger. Did you take the medicine I gave you regularly, every hour?"

Mr. Beranger took a small green phial from his pocket, and drank some of its contents.

After some more conversation, they both retired to the mysterious locked-up chamber, as was their wont. I had occasion to pass it, and beheld Madame Mellitton with her ear to the keyhole. "Haywan!" muttered she, in a deep voice, and what a word of ineffable scorn "Haywan!" must be in her language.

One day when I was sitting with a book in my hand, thinking of Miss Ryder and Oxford, she came and sat down beside me.

"You often read," said she, "and still I think you are not a bookworm. I think you would prefer being something else than a tutor."

"Perhaps you are right," said I. "What makes you think so?"

"A bookworm is never preoccupied," replied she; "he never dreams or sleeps over his book, and he never holds it upside down."

I started with a blush, for mine was in that position.

"Do not turn it, Mr. Gessler," smiled she. "I want to speak to you."

She then began to make close inquiries, relative to my birth, parentage, education, etc. Madame Mellitton must have had some important reason for her inquisitiveness in these matters, for she was particularly desirous to know how my acquaintance with Mr. Beranger had originated, and if I knew Colonel Ryder. My heart beat fast, and I turned to her eagerly.

"Do you know Colonel Ryder?" said I.

"I am the worst person in the world to ask questions of," replied she. "I have an old habit of never answering them. What should I know of Colonel Ryder any more than you?"

"I thought because you spoke of him," said I.

"I sometimes speak of subjects as uninteresting to me as the weather or the crops," said she, with a hard smile.

"Will you not tell me how Miss Castellon is?" said I.

"What do you care for Miss Castellon?" inquired she. "If she were to die you would only say 'poor creature!'"

Her dark eyes streamed fire.

"I have a most sincere friendship for her," said I.

"Pshaw!" cried she, "I do not believe in friendship."

And after working a few moments in silence, she gathered her cambric web together and went out.

That very evening Mr. Beranger was smitten with a strange and serious illness, half a trance and half an ague. He was borne to bed, and lay there in a terrible state. The muscles were sometimes rigid, then they would quiver into convulsive motion. The sharp white teeth would gnash then upon us, as he ground them spasmodically till the foam whitened on his livid lips. I thought the attack resembled epilepsy. I found Dr. Mustapha sitting cross-legged at the patient's bedroom fire, calmly smoking.

"Is the illness fatal?" inquired I, eagerly.

"Always," answered he, caressing his moustaches.

"What is it?" said I. "How did it begin? What is its name?"

"It is one of our diseases," said he, very slowly. "The great national disease, the great national infatuation and curse, the doom of——" (then followed a Turkish word.

"What is its name?" interrogated I.

He uttered a foreign word.

"That is the name in Arabic," said he. "It has no equivalent in English; or, stay, Bismillah, I think it has."

"Do pray explain the disease to me," said I, imploringly.

"Can you cure it?" inquired he, solemnly, lifting his eyes.

"No, alas! no," answered I. "I wish I could."

"Then," said he, "your question is idle and useless, and my answer would be idle and useless also. May I trouble you, Effendi, to fling more fuel on the fire?"

I moved quietly and noiselessly over to the coal-skuttle.

"You need not go so softly," cried the philosophic doctor. "Allah be praised, he won't hear you."

"Will you do nothing more for the recovery of the patient?" said I.

Mustapha trimmed the fire, and then replied,

"Say, '*can* you do anything more for the recovery of the patient?' and I will answer 'No.' Bismillah, Effendi, when a mortal reaches a certain distance to the gates of death, he cannot be brought back. Let me throw this fragrant herb on the fire. I have known them to have the sense of smell at this stage; let it burn."

This phlegm was peculiarly distressing to me, under the circumstances; there sat the old gentleman, cross-legged, calmly snuffing in the warm and delicious perfume exhaled from the burning root, apparently thinking nothing about Mr. Beranger.

"Let me summon an English physician," said I.

This proposition seemed to excite the indignation of the Eastern physician.

"I have attended a Vizier," cried he, "a Grand Vizier, who had this disease. Blessed be the Prophet! he died; and no great loss to the nation either, for a greater tyrant never died under the bow-string. Call in an English leech, who will treat this as a native disease, and our friend will never rise again."

"Will he rise again, then?" inquired I.

"Bismillah! no."

And he drew his legs closer together.

"Then he will never recover?" said I, sadly.

"This is what you call June—the time of your roses?" said he.

"Yes," replied I.

The Mussulman wiped his amber mouthpiece.

"Well, then," said he, "when your roses go away, he will be dead. But we will remember him, Effendi; for his memory will be to us like those perfumes which linger for ages. Do you perceive that odour? It is like a breath from a Turkish bower!"

And the cool old heathen snuffed up his beloved odour again.

"You will regret him; you will be sorry for him," said I. "The loss of a friend is a great loss."

"There is one God, and Mohammet is his Prophet!" said he. "His will be done. This is an evil world, and Paradise is the abode of the blessed."

The pious Turkish philosopher uttered these words (doubtless from the Koran) as passionlessly as he would read an extract from "Bradshaw's Guide" or "Murray's Time Table."

Madame Mellitton entered the room. Her face was deadly pale; her teeth were visible between her parted lips, which were white with dread and excitement. She approached the bed, and looked on Mr. Beranger. She and Dr. Mustapha then conferred together in their own language, she wildly and hotly, and he with his accustomed coolness and phlegm. Then she shook the patient, as if to wake him, and shouted some words in his ear. The doctor smiled at these efforts, which produced no effect on Mr. Beranger.

"Death is surely Beranger's kismet now, at any rate!" cried the doctor, in English, to get another hearer of his wit. "The Sultan himself could not command a word out of him. No wonder that there are no women in Paradise!"

Madame Mellitton addressed some native words to him—sharp, guttural, and angry—with a snarl like that of a lioness; but Mustapha laughed at them behind a cloud of tobacco-smoke.

"The patient appears to suffer," said I. "If the disease cannot be cured, can you not alleviate the pain?"

The physician slowly approached the bed, wiped away the froth from the sick man's lips, and then applied a phial to his lips and nostrils. Something like the animation of healthy life broke over Mr. Beranger's face at each inspiration of the liquid; the warm blood seemed to circulate more freely, the rigid muscles became relaxed, and his sleep was no longer restless and agitated; his breathing was calm and composed as that of a child. It seemed the work of a happy necromancy. I was in an ecstasy of hope; but Mustapha merely shrugged his shoulders, and said "Haywan!" I remembered the word as that which Madame Mellitton had uttered at the door of Mr. Beranger's mysterious chamber.

"What does 'Haywan mean?" said I.

"'Fool!'" replied Mustapha; "and you are a fool to be transported at that deceptive and artificial sleep. It is the last blaze of the rocket; it will darken by and by for ever."

I went to my own apartments, and wrote the sad news to Pietro Wells, as I thought he ought to know all before any catastrophe occurred. While I was writing, Madame Muscat entered, with the most wonderful head-dress I had ever seen. After weeping downright deluges of tears, she gave me a lengthened detail of all she knew about Mr. Beranger.

His parents had been English, she said, but he was born and bred in some foreign country, and the predilections and antipathies of his far-away home clung to him yet. His only British peculiarities were a liking for port and sherry, and a bantering manner of talking about women never heard out of England, or, at any rate (as if correcting herself), never heard in France. But then he was so wealthy, so generous, so courteous (and here the tears flowed in torrents); besides, he was the most exquisite and unique dresser in London; and to think that such a man was about to die!

"Mon Dieu!" faltered Madame, "it must be a mistake; I cannot believe the dark gentleman. What should Monsieur Beranger die for?"

This speech came out in gasps, through her hands and her white handkerchief. I uttered all the words of condolence I could think of, although Madame Muscat, with her remarkable head-dress, was by no means a tempting subject for experimental consolation. Suddenly looking me in the face, she exclaimed—

"Is Madame Mellitton sane?"

"I have every reason for thinking she is," answered I.

"So had I, until Monsieur's illness," said she. "But now she sits on a chair for hours at a time, with her hands locked together, and her eyes fixed; then she leaps up in a moment, rushes to Monsieur's bed, and screams and shouts in his ears. Mon Dieu! what is she? where did she come from?"

I did not chose to enlighten Madame on these points.

For some days Mr. Beranger lay in the state I have described—calm, and sometimes apparently conscious, but dumb, sleepless, and pale. He seemed to understand some of the comforting words addressed to him, but he never spoke. One day Mr. Leer summoned me to the sick chamber, to put my signature to the Will; Mr. Tamper was there also, and Philip Marr was the other witness to the deed. I rejoiced at this opportunity of seeing Mr. Beranger once more, and of bidding him farewell. I went over to the bedside, and took his hand; and as I was struggling with my emotions while endeavouring to utter the word "Farewell," he opened his eyes, and gazed at me with an expression that showed he was conscious both of my presence and sympathy. The eyelids then fell.

When I looked round, I saw that Philip

Marr had been standing beside me, with his eyes fixed on the sick man. How many coincidences occur in life! Mr. Tamper beckoned me to the table, and with palsied hand and dimmed eyes I placed my name on the swimming paper. Some drops of ink unfortunately fell from my pen.

"Young man," said Mr. Leer, severely, "the grief which interferes with the humblest duty is improper—improper!"

His eyes glared at me from under his glasses. Philip Marr and I had not an opportunity of exchanging one word together, for he went away immediately after the signing of the Will. Small incidents like this sometimes decide one's fate; at least, they did mine.

When I left the bedroom, I found Madame Mellitton standing outside the door. Deep anxiety was written on her face.

"Is there no hope of his recovery?" said she, with eagerness and emotion. "Will he pass away thus dumb and dormant; without sense and faculty; never hearing, speaking, or understanding again?"

"Dr. Mustapha fears so, Madame," said I.

" He knows the malady well, and asserts that he will not outlive the night."

She turned her head away with a groan.

" Mustapha gave no hope," said she, hoarsely, after a time. " He is sure to die then, for he has said it."

She moved away, and then returned again.

" On your honour!" cried she, " you aver that what you have said is truth? You do not deceive me? You think anyone would be a stranger to him now—anyone?"

" Madame," said I, earnestly, " Be assured that what I have stated is true. You cannot suppose I would deceive you, especially at a moment like this."

She grasped my hand in both hers.

" Mr. Gessler," said she, " you will have more frequent opportunities of seeing the patient than I; Mustapha will not watch you. When the least sign of sense or consciousness returns, come to me, lose not a moment, come at any hour, do not fear that I shall be asleep. I have not undressed or slept since his illness, nor will I until he is dead. You will promise me this?"

I did promise her, and she thanked me with earnestness.

I went out for my customary stroll up and down before the house; my anxiety about Mr. Beranger would not permit me to stray farther. I had not been long out when a most disreputable-looking cab stopped at the door. A head was thrust out of the window, and I almost gasped for breath when, the door being opened, Pietro Wells stepped out. The poor usher knew me at once, and falling upon my neck, he lifted up his voice and wept.

"Take me to him!" cried he, sorrowfully; "take me to him; I did not think it would have come to this. Is there really no hope?"

I tried to prevail upon him to take some rest and refreshment after his journey, but he only turned from me and wailed.

"Take me to him; in the name of *your* God take me to him!"

It was no time to stand and ask him why He was not *his* also. I led him upstairs, and knocked at the sick man's chamber door. Dr. Mustapha, who always prowled about it like a black guardian, met us on the threshold. I repeated the usher's request to him. Before he could reply, Wells exclaimed—

"Hassan, Hassan, a look at you brings me home, and makes me young once more. I think I hear the College chimes striking again, and the boys laughing and shouting. Give me your hand, and let me feel that we are together once more."

"Bismillah!" cried Mustapha, smiling. "You are mad yet, Pietro. How many books have you read since we met? Allah! be praised; I only know learning by name. Come in, come in, and have a smoke!"

"Does he sleep, Hassan?" said Wells, approaching the bed. "Wake him, I must speak to him; I have not many words to say, only a few, and farewell. Wake him!"

"It is vain," said Mustapha; "he is an instrument without one string; he will never speak or hear again—he cannot even bid you farewell. Go quickly, and look your last on him; for he will never hear your great bells toll another hour."

Pietro Wells rushed to the bedside with a cry of grief, and kneeling down, he wept over the sick man.

"Albert!" said he, "Albert! Albert! you do not know me now, bût I am Pietro! You forget it all now, Albert, don't you?—and you forgive them all? You remember what I wrote you about Edmund and Mercia?"

"Hush!" cried Mr. Beranger, to our astonishment rising suddenly, and waving his hand. "Leave us alone all of you. Mustapha, close the door; let none enter here."

His long-hushed voice sounded wondrously firm and clear. I shall long remember the startling effect produced by what I may almost call the return to life of that prostrate form, and the sudden recovery of the power of speech.

Pietro Wells remained a considerable time alone with Mr. Beranger, I think for some hours, during which Dr. Mustapha, with a pipe in his mouth, strode up and down the long corridor. I saw Madame Mellitton, and fulfilled my promise; she came to the bedroom door, where she and her countryman had one of their usual parleys, which ended (as they always ended) in the lady's defeat. I went straight to Baptist's apartments, and, shocked to find him painting, I said to him very severely—

"Mr. Beranger is dying. Do you not wish to see him once more? You had better come down this moment."

"He is in a state of coma, is he not?" replied he. "It is too late for him to do me justice now; he carries away the secret of my birth into the home of silence. I shall never know a mother's love, if she exists; or her grave, if she is dead. He goes away, and leaves me alone."

"He was conscious a few minutes ago," said I, "and I heard him speak. Perhaps you may not yet be too late."

He ran down stairs hastily, and I followed him; he approached the door, and impatiently demanded admittance. Dr. Mustapha approached, and told him that he could not allow any one to enter at that moment.

"How dare you thus become gaoler of the dying?" said Baptist, angrily. "Out of my way, man, I must see him."

Dr. Mustapha listened for a moment at the door, and then opened it; Baptist pressed in after him, followed by Madame Mellitton and myself. As the eastern doctor hastily entered he went close to the sick man, and uttered the word "Shemdi." Mr. Beranger was lying back, fixed and white; Pietro Wells was kneeling by the bed-side, his head buried in the clothes; the one as silent and motionless as the other. Mustapha gave one glance at the sick man, and then, turning round to us with raised arms, as if to command silence, he solemnly said,—

"Dead! he is dead."

"Impossible!" cried Baptist, passionately. "It is a falsehood, a wrong, he is not dead; people with tales to tell like his do not die silent. Back, man, or, by heaven, I will strike you down!"

"Say all this to Allah," said Dr. Mustapha, calmly, "and he will answer you, but the dead and the living cannot. Lay not a hand upon the body, it is *my* dead, for I love it, and I dare you to touch it. Bismillah! look and tell me if *that* is life."

We all gazed on Mr. Beranger. Although, death being so recent, an expression something like that of life still lingered on his countenance, yet no one could doubt that Mr. Beranger was now at rest. Madame Mellitton approached the usher, who turned round, and stared her in the face.

"Pietro, dear Pietro," said she, "remember what I am, and welcome me back again."

"Ay!" replied he, bitterly. "I thought you would be here; I never saw ruin or misery without you. What sin did you come for now? Not against Albert, for you cannot cheat him again. Take away your hand; the wrong you did to him yesterday—it was yesterday, was it not?" He put his hand to his head, as if to arrest his wandering thoughts.

"Not yesterday," said Madame Mellitton, "but twenty-two years ago; remember the date, and let it weaken your displeasure. If I did any wrong, he returned it tenfold, as you know. Pietro, for the sake of that tie which is between us, look at me, and give me your hand."

"Do not urge it, woman," cried the usher, rising in a fury; "the tie is nothing.

The bonds of blood are between the strangers that love each other, not between the brethren that hate. Go away, go away! Youth is gone, and Albert is gone; dead, with no other world to go to!" He threw himself down by the bed again, and wept till all emotion and memory seemed to pass away with his tears. When I raised him up he was himself again. Madame Mellitton's eyes glowed with a passion to which she gave no expression in language. She spoke some words to Mustapha in Turkish, which sounded like an inquiry, but he only shook his head disdainfully. With a long, searching gaze at Baptist and at me, she then left the room, Mustapha's twinkling eyes following her to the door with a glance in which there was an expression at once sardonic and humorous. Then he stroked his beard, and growing solemn and pompous, he turned towards Baptist, and said,—

"Away! I must honour the dead; you would find no life there although you were to watch for ever. Your wishes or your prayers can never bring back a spirit. He is as a stone dropped into the ocean, that can never be found again, he will never return. Peace be with him!"

Without another word Baptist left the room. Poor Wells seemed stupefied as he sat staring stonily at the table lamp. He had been sitting on a chair by the window, and, placing his chin in his hand, had contemplated the last rays of red sunlight till they faded out, and the moonlight till the curtains hid it; then he confined his glance to the flame of oil, till I, with much difficulty, persuaded him to retire for the night. How dreadfully vacant, yet how fearfully tenanted, a house with the dead has always seemed to me! That familiar room, which I had whistled past many a time, was now, to me at least, invested with a weird awe, a breathless reverence, and darkened by the shadow of the angel of Death. To rid myself of painful emotions, and for a time to forget my own thoughts in those of others, I had recourse to a book, when Selim entered with a wary step, and glanced wistfully, nay, suspiciously, all round the room.

"Well, Selim," said I, "have you lost anything?"

He gave a sigh of relief, and crept close to me.

"Then it didn't come in here, sir?" said he.

"What do you mean?" exclaimed I.

He spoke in a whisper.

"I saw something long and grey walking through the house," said he. "It comed up-stairs, and it must have gone past here."

"Nonsense, Selim," answered I.

"No, it ain't nonsense, sir," exclaimed Selim, sharply; "and you'll find that out when you're long in these 'ere rooms. Hush! it's going past!"

I listened silently, and heard a species of stealthy, rustling sound, like a muffled footstep, and a bated breath, passing the door, behind which Selim crouched I placed my hand on his shoulder, and felt his entire frame quaking.

"Selim!" said I, "what is that?"

"I don't know; nobody," he said, with a sharp tone, between a snap and a whine. "I don't know nothin'; don't never ask me nothin'."

"Why, what's the matter?" exclaimed I,

amazed at these dark and obscure sayings.

"Pish!" replied Selim, snappishly. "I never knows the matter of nothin', and sometimes, when it comes on dark, I hopes I never shall! But if you does, sir, foller me." He rose up, and, keeping close to the wall, crept swiftly and cautiously along the corridor, I wending my way after him. It was a long passage, lighted here and there by a stray moonbeam, or a lamp, and I traced his progress by the white or yellow flicker which rested now and then on his muslin turban. Then he suddenly bent down behind a pillar, and sat there perfectly still, with all his snowy vesture darkened by the shadow of the statue. I came up with him, and beheld Madame Mellitton—clothed in a long grey dress, standing with her ear at the bedroom door. Its only occupants were one living and one dead man—Dr. Mustapha and Mr. Beranger—yet the expression of her face, as the lamp fell upon it, was that of one who had heard something by which she was profoundly moved.

END OF FIRST BOOK.

BOOK THE SECOND.

FLORIAN AND MISS RYDER.

CHAPTER VI.

A DREAM REALIZED AND SHATTERED.—A QUARREL. —A NEW ENGAGEMENT.

"O sovereign power of love! O grief! O balm!"
Keats.

NEXT morning when the sun rose, Pietro Wells, through the sheer force of habit, rose also, for he was never known to lie abed after the luxurious hour of five in the morning. He seemed considerably amazed at the flood of sunshine which bathed him as he rose; for the almost Cimmerian darkness of the lane in Oxford had impressed him with the belief that nature was a niggard of her light and sunshine. When I met him shortly after, he addressed me in his usual abrupt way.

"Well, well!" said he. "I'm not at

Oxford; it's amazing! This is London, you say; can the British Museum be seen from this? I have begun to wear glasses since I saw you last—where are they? I put them in my bag. Where is my bag, Mr. Gessler?"

"You did not bring one, Mr. Wells," said I; "you only brought this book," and I gave him his old classic.

"Great Jove! what an ass I am!" cried he. "I remember now, I put the bag filled with necessaries for my journey on the table, and Euripides beside it; I clutched Euripides (how glad I am that I did so!) and left the bag. Do not look sorry, Mr. Gessler; the exchange is excellent. I took away golden thoughts, and left old shirts."

"But you cannot read Euripides without glasses," said I. "I will instantly get you a pair."

"I could repeat Euripides from beginning to end, although I were blind," said the old usher, with a smile.

"Better that you had taken the bag, then," said I.

"No, better that I had taken that last monkish MS. which I bought yesterday," sighed he, "it throws a new light on the doctrine of Pythagoras; but your letter threw me into such a state that I forgot everything. Would you believe it, Mr. Gessler; I tore a leaf out of Horace, to light my candle; I regret the foolish mistake. Albert Mercia Hassan! dead; another part of the great nothingness which lies beyond the tomb!—dead, a cinder, —dust and ashes; a thing, a substance (if Pythagoras tells us truly) that will go to make up a dog or a cat!"

"What opinions are these, Mr. Wells?" said I, gravely.

"The true!" exclaimed he, laying his hand on my arm. "I have two opinions which ye would all flout at, but they lie speechless in my breast, like treasures in the sea; but some waves wash them up. Monarchy is the best kind of slavery in the world, and Christianity is the best delusion in the universe. I despise crowns and I disbelieve creeds, but be a subject and a Christian; remember that!"

These words made me almost recoil from him with horror, but then I thought of the poor old man, enfeebled by sorrow and study, and fooled by his very learning into error, and pitied him. I therefore answered, gravely,

"Mr. Wells, have you ever read the simple old-world story on which this delusion was founded? Did you ever hear of that man who died one day on a cross near Jerusalem? I have no argument against you but that life; read it and remember it."

"Yes!" cried he, clasping his hands; "the tale is beautiful, sublime, touching in its simplicity; it is the grandest I have ever read. It was written by a master hand, Mr. Gessler; Virgil could not have written it; I tell you that one of the ancients could not have come near it; the language is exquisite, the style natural, the plot a glorious conception. Believe it all as much as the martyrs believed it. Its morality is the purest ever conceived; I have kept all its commandments but one,—do you keep them all; and believe every word of it in letter and spirit, for I would like you to believe it all."

"Do not attempt to teach me again," said I, severely; "I will never be a moral infidel, say what you will."

"I did not tell *you* that, did I?" said he, in the tone of one awakened from a sleep. "I hope I didn't,—I hope I didn't!"

His face wore the most miserable expression it could assume, and the tone of his voice denoted so much suffering, that I thought it cruel to pursue the conversation farther.

"Do you think he is actually dead?" said he, at breakfast.

"Alas! there is no doubt of it," replied I.

"Did he die with words of anger and hatred?" muttered he. "What did he say? ah!—'Curses on them, Pietro, my death will not be my forgiveness, but my vengeance.' That was strange, for he cannot move a finger now, or whisper a word."

Selim at that moment came to tell me that "the Colonel, which was Mr. Beranger's nearest relation, had comed, and that Madame Muscat wanted me for to go and meet him, as she was 'isterics all over, and couldn't leave her bed, and didn't think she ever should." Now, as I had never been a 'family man,' I was perfectly unaccustomed to doing the honours of any establishment; therefore I fled down stairs for Mr. Trickem, knowing that he, as master of the courtesies of private life, could discharge this duty with the "easier grace." I found this gentleman and the cook strengthening their nervous systems, in the laundry, with an exhilarating beverage, which they, in the manner of free translators, termed a "decoction for the nerves," but which, to my notion, resembled nothing so much as pale brandy. Abandoning, therefore, my idea of making Mr. Trickem do the honours of the house in my stead, and armed with as much composure as I could muster, I went upstairs to do the honours. The Colonel stood on the door step superintending, with a haughty military air, the removal of his luggage from the cab to the house. His aspect was as severely martial as his voice; had he been mailed from head to heel, and armed to the teeth, it scarcely could have been more so. He was elderly, tall and stout, broad-chested, and with a great deal of moustache; his whole appearance betokening the "military man."

"Can I assist you in any way, sir?" said I, bowing.

He measured me from head to foot with his eye, which was as bright and blue as steel.

"I thank you," replied he. "May I ask who you are?"

"The tutor," answered I; "Mr. Baptist's tutor."

"And who, may I ask, is Mr. Baptist?" inquired he.

"Mr. Beranger's nephew," returned I.

He started with surprise.

"Nephew!" echoed he, "nephew! that is very strange!" He mused a moment, and then bit his lip, to conceal a smile. Then turning to the cabman, he said, "Cabman, take care of that fowling-piece and that valise."

A tall young lady and gentleman entered, followed by a little limping boy, for whom I opened the white drawing-room door.

"Thank you, you are very kind," said the young lady, in the sweetest and clearest tones that *I* ever heard, or shall ever hear again. As she passed, she gave me a furtive glance, from eyes of the most beautiful blue I had ever beheld.

"Florian!" cried the little limping boy, pulling her dress, and pointing to a statue of Pysche. "Florian, look at that pretty white angel with the pitcher."

"Yes, dear," said Florian, looking back; and our eyes again met. "How beautiful it is!"

Then they went in, and it was with a feeling of agony, almost of despair, that I watched one of the three figures as they entered the white chamber, for was not Mr. Beranger's heiress, Florian, Philip Marr's bethrothed wife, and Miss Ryder, my Oxford love?

This was the bitter story of Tantalus. Again the water was close to my lips, but I could not touch it. I could never, never tell my love to Florian now; my affection must perish in the bud, my thoughts must live unuttered. Fate had made her at once everything and nothing to me. We had met too late; better, then, that we had never met at all. The treasure which I had sighed, prayed, hoped, and yearned for, many long years, was now in my grasp, but my hand dared not close upon it. I had to yield it up to another. The young gentleman, Captain Ryder, came out of the drawing-room and accosted me. I tried to command myself and address him with words of courtesy, hoping they were not fatigued by their journey, and that they would not scruple to command my services in any way that would conduce to their comfort, etc.

"We hadn't a very long journey of it," said he, frankly and pleasantly, "only a run up from Oxford; and we do not feel fatigued in the least, with the exception of my brother who is ill, and a little wearied out. But I suppose (he continued with a merry light in his eyes) you never acted as Abigail to a lady, therefore, if you would send a chamber-maid to my sister, or some one of that description, I should feel obliged."

"Francis!" cried at this moment the most musical voice in the world, "Francis!"

Florian observed me and went hastily back. I hastened to summon a domestic, while Captain Ryder entered the dining-room.

Francis Ryder was a man whom anyone

would admire. He always made a great impression in public, and distinguished himself everywhere. He had that peculiar manner which at once prepossessed others in his favour, and invited their confidence. There was something in the expression of his countenance, the glance of his eye, the tone of his voice, that at once fascinated all who associated with him. He was very tall and proportionably stout, the symmetry of his form reminding one of some of the more perfect ancient statues. The chest was broad, massive, and deep, and his head and face were beautiful, the features being at once manly and regular. The hair was of a pale soft auburn, cut in true military style. The eyes were large and soft, and of a deep dark blue, the brow fair, wide, and tranquil. Candour, good humour, tenderness, benevolence, and refinement were diffused over his whole countenance. He had many admirers, warm ones too, but my admiration rose almost to enthusiasm. Nor when we grew intimate, and I came to know his little faults and imperfections, did it at all diminish. His candour often led him into scrapes, and his wit cost him frequent quarrels; his benevolence was sometimes hasty and misdirected; his refinement drew him into luxury, and his luxury into extravagance; his tenderness was so universal that it sometimes assumed the appearance of fickleness; and the softness of his features might be supposed to betoken a want of energy. But he possessed other virtues which were free from all defect and imperfection—a high sense of honour, an unflinching bravery, a pure morality, a genial temper, and a sunny disposition. Whatever errors or follies the world's temptation and pleasure led him into, these virtues were ever the conspicuous ornaments of his character, His conversation was a perpetual volley of small shot, very pleasant and bewitching to listen to. I wish I could faithfully transcribe some portions of his conversation; but that would be impossible,—his wit, excellent as it undoubtedly was, owing so much to the peculiar manner that rendered his conversation so attractive to all who listened to him.

Dr. Mustapha's entrance interrrupted my reveries.

"You are Captain Ryder, I believe," said he, bowing low with oriental courtesy, yet with a queer twinkle in his eye. "I am an old friend, although you know it not; your father knows Hassan Mustapha well. Bismillah! I burn to see him; and there is his voice."

The fine tones of the Colonel sounded at that moment; he soon after entered the room, and Mustapha leaping forward to meet him, grasped his hands, chattering in Turkish the whole time.

The Colonel by no means relished or reciprocated this cordial friendship; he merely drew himself up and stared.

"Can any of you make this person understand," said Colonel Ryder, severely, "that I neither know himself nor his language; and that I am not the old friend whom his words and actions would imply?"

And he frowned and expanded his chest majestically.

"Bismillah! I know your English well enough!" said Mustapha, grinning somewhat spitefully; "and I know *you;* memory sees plenty old familiar things in you yet. Wonderful that you do not know me; I was Hassan the beardless then, but look at me now. Still I am Hassan. Perhaps you will not know Beranger when you see him to-morrow."

The Colonel moved uneasily.

"But," continued the Turk, humorously, yet with some feeling of bitterness, "I might have recollected that you always had a bad memory where old friends were concerned. I am glad we meet as we parted; I poor and you rich. I wish you happiness."

The Colonel looked as if he would bluster and hector; but ere he could say a word Mustapha walked out of the apartment.

"A strange old fox that," said Francis. "He looks ugly enough in a passion, but I like him better bitter than cordial. Do you know him, sir?"

The Colonel glanced at me and hemmed with severity.

"Francis," said he, with dignity, "you will visit Mr. Philip Marr to-night, and acquaint him with the change, I mean with the increase to our fortune, caused by the lamented death of Mr. Beranger. You will present him my compliments, and say how happy I—we all—shall be to see him visiting here on the old footing. Your sister is writing a note to him, which you will get from her before you leave; you will find him in the office of Messrs. Tamper and Leer. Where is it now?"

"In Lincoln's Inn," said I. "I know it well."

The Colonel disdained to acknowledge or answer this, but continued—

"Or in his residence, the address of which you know; I wish him to be present at the solemn ceremony of to-morrow, as he is virtually, if not really, a member of the family."

"Poor Philip!" cried Francis, warmly, "he is the finest fellow in the world; but rather dull and prosy."

"Dull!" echoed his father, frowning. "He is a talented and intellectual man; these are the qualifications which have gained him my esteem; otherwise—" he paused.

"Intellect is always so heavy!" laughed Francis; "although I have never felt its weight personally. But I think I shall go to him this minute. Do you know him?"

"Very intimately," answered I.

The Colonel raised his eyebrows.

"We were together at Oxford," explained I.

"Then you will come with me," exclaimed Francis, rising.

I followed him; like Goethe's Faust, my whole being beat like one mighty pulse, for I knew that I should find Florian in the drawing-room.

She sat by the table with a pen in her small, slender, white hand; she had been writing. I gazed at her earnestly, for even under all the sad circumstances of the case, it was a delight for me to behold her. She was a subdued reflection of her brother. The calm aquiline features—the broad soft blue eye—the pale auburn hair, braided on the white brow and the fair cheek; the contour of the tall graceful form, the tone of the low, clear voice, her very manner of expressing sorrow and joy—all were his. Yet despite the close resemblance, she was not beautiful; with all the grace of youth, her one prominent charm was simplicity. The only quality by which she fascinated others was her goodness. There were also differences of character between the brother and sister. Florian's disposition was not so ardent as that of Francis. Extreme delicacy and purity of heart are capable of calm, quiet affection, but not of hot, impulsive passion. Francis would reason too little and sacrifice too much for love, while Florian would reason too much and sacrifice too little. Like her brother, she was rather infirm of purpose, and easily influenced by others; her love for her father and brothers was deep, intense, and absorbing; and these two qualities, weakness of purpose and strength of love, led her into the self-sacrificing error which was the ruin and misery of her own life, and of all that loved her. But I will leave the future to tell its own story. Francis presented me to her; she gave me one long look of welcome, and then turning away her beautiful eyes, blushed with emotion. Her hand lay in mine longer than courtésy demanded, as if by that act she wished to indicate that the dream of our love might yet be realized in a real union; then sitting down again on her seat she played with the pen.

"We are going to Philip, Florian," said the captain. "Is your letter finished yet? You have been writing it for the last hour. Come, let me have it."

"I have written nothing," said she, in a low voice. "Only the date; you cannot take him that, Frank."

"Where is the eloquence of love, Florian," said he, "when it is not able to fill a half sheet of note-paper?"

This badinage seemed to give her pain; her cheek reddened.

"Let me be eloquent some other way," said she. "I am a poor correspondent; words fly from me, and I must speak my thoughts without them."

Our eyes met (not by chance, but by design), and the pulse of my being throbbed again hotly and madly; she seemed to remember all our long silent love, and how little it had ever owed to language either spoken or written, and the blush which on my entrance had tinged her cheek, now deepened. Francis turned to address me,—

"You are very silent, Mr. Gessler."

"I am very fond of silence," replied I; "circumstances have made it dearer to me than speech."

I paused, and dared not look this time towards the table.

What we had both for years thirsted to say to each other was spoken; the secret of our hearts was at last revealed. Philip Marr, the lover and the friend, had been forgotten for one moment and remembered in the next. But henceforth, if we would be honourable, we must be silent; silent not only in word, but even in the language spoken by a glance of the eye, or a smile on the lip. That silence which united us before must separate us now. Florian again played idly with her pen, as if she cared not to write. A thrill of delight swept through my soul (for there is no being so selfish as the lover); it was evident that she did not love Philip, and that thought to me was unutterable rapture.

"You knew the—you knew Mr. Beranger?" said Florian, suddenly.

"I knew him," replied I, "but not well; he was not a man to be known well. He did not seem to care for friendship."

Francis had gone to a distant window; Florian looked after him, and then, bending forward to me, spoke earnestly and hurriedly.

"Without knowing him," said she, "what instinctive impression would he be apt to make?"

"I scarcely know how to answer you, Miss Ryder," replied I. "I was a stranger to Mr. Beranger, and it is scarcely fair to judge a human being by the impulse of a first impression, which a more intimate acquaintance with him and a deeper knowledge of his character might have dissipated altogether; and seeing now that I can never know him better, I dare not tell you the impression."

"It is not a good one, by your hesitation," said Florian; "but whatever it is, pray tell it to me; and grant the first favour I ever asked you." She bent her head; and the sun shone upon her hair and the delicate hand that rested on the blank sheet of white paper.

"The first impression which Mr. Beranger

made upon me," said I, "was singular and unaccountable."

"In what respect, Mr. Gessler?" interrogated she.

"We were strangers, as I said before," continued I. "I never knew of his existence till the moment in which we met, and yet the impression was a painful one, even repulsive."

"And did that feeling," asked she, "ever pass away?"

"Never!" replied I. "Remember, I grant you your first favour; or I would never have disclosed this to you or anyone."

"I understand you," said she, "and thank you. If no circumstances ever weakened this impression, did ever any occur that strengthened it?" Her eyes remained keenly fixed on me.

"Yes," answered I, "it deepened daily; his very kindness and humour deepened it. I am ungrateful to say so, but some feelings can never be shaken away; Mr. Beranger was very kind to me."

"He was very kind to you," echoed she, thoughtfully. "You must have doubted its sincerity, then, or you would not shrink from it! Did you think him insincere?"

"Not exactly," answered I; "it was not from his visible acts and words that I shrank, but from those which I did not see or hear. It was not himself that I disliked, but the mystery—the deception—which was a part of him."

She almost started, and her cheek fired.

"What deception, what mystery, do you refer to, Mr. Gessler?" cried she. "How do you know that he deceived?"

"My answer will show you the folly of these impressions, Miss Ryder," said I. "I never had the slightest proof that Mr. Beranger was insincere and deceptive."

"What circumstances did you allude to before?" inquired she; "I mean those which deepened your unfavourable impression."

"These were foolish and trivial, also," said I. "He had a small secret chamber, the interior of which no one had ever seen; he used to spend hours there, and come out pale and ghastly. He also took frequent journeys to some unknown place; to woo a lady, he said."

"These things only prove him to be mysterious," said Florian, growing crimson. "Mystery is sometimes a holy and virtuous thing."

At this moment Francis approached us. "I was just watching an ass of a fellow, who was trying all he could to break his neck on horseback!" said he. "Where is your epistle, Florian? By Jupiter! not a word yet. Come away, Mr. Gessler; Philip is generally at home just now."

Florian and I shook hands; our eyes are seldom our slaves, else our glances would not have met again.

We found Philip Marr at home; he was lying on a sofa, with a heated and throbbing brow, after the morning's exertions. He grasped a hand of each with warm cordiality.

"Well, Ryder, I am delighted to see you," said he, "if you do not bear bad news. How are all at home? How is Florian? Were you at Oxford?"

"Quite well, old fellow," said Francis. "Sit down again, and cool yourself, you seem as red and weary as a galley slave. We have not been better or happier at home for years."

"Well, what has happened, Frank?" said he; "you look big with something which seems like glad tidings."

Then Francis sat beside him, and told him all the story of the fortune, how Mr. Beranger's lawyers had written to the Colonel as the principal heir, to come and take immediate possession of the house, and to hear the Will read.

Philip listened with quiet interest, but whether he was delighted or depressed his countenance did not show.

"We are no longer equals then," said he; "you are rich and I am poor; the great gulf lies between us, Frank, and you stand on the bright, and I on the dark side."

"Don't talk nonsense, Phil," cried Francis; "you surely know what fast friends the Ryders make in storm and shine—and Florian of course."

Philip raised himself up quickly and suddenly.

"It is a pity fortune has meddled with

her," cried he, sadly and quietly; "it is a pity that she was not left poor."

"I say, Marr," exclaimed Francis, "don't talk such confounded stuff, I have no patience with it. What the deuce (you *will* force me to swear)—what the deuce makes you doubt Florian, and speak of her as if she were a fortune-hunter or a coquette?"

"You are all in London now, I believe?" exclaimed Marr.

"Every one of us," said Francis; "get your hat, Phil, and let us be off!"

"You forget how footsore and weary I am," replied Philip, smiling. "I have walked through the hot, noisy streets, and been cramped up in a stifling office all day. I have numberless papers to write, and am thirsty and drowsy. I cry your mercy, sir!"

"We will get into a fly, and reach home in time for luncheon," said Francis. "What will Florian think, old fellow?—you speak as if you were a free man, and not in the bonds of love. Now, I consider courtship the greatest slavery in the world. When I'm in love, I have not a moment that I can call my own, from morning till night, with a charming slave-driver over me. But you will soon be free, old fellow, as there is no liberty but marriage for this description of bondmen."

Francis was always making jokes on this subject, but Philip was firm in his determination; decision was one of his characteristics; he arranged his parchments and writing materials on the table.

"And you are resolved not to see Florian to-night," said Francis. "I envy you,—you are a cold lover."

A certain expression as of pain or scorn covered the young lawyer's face.

"Florian knows me sufficiently well," said he, "to excuse my not seeing her to night; you accuse me of coldness, but I assure you I feel heated enough just now."

"You are beginning to look like a lover at last," said Francis; "we shall have a happy marriage in St. George's soon. I hope you have given up your morbid affection for country chapels and parish churches, and for curates with all the interest of poverty about them. Get spliced in Hanover Square, old fellow, by a regular fat bishop."

Mr. Marr smiled, and a glow of joy swept over his face; but it was only the rapture of a moment's forgetfulness; for he leaned his head on his hand, and became thoughtful. Then, after a pause, he said—

"So you are to leave pretty Ivy-nook Cottage, for this nabob's London palace?—but perhaps you will feel as sad as I did, in exchanging home for this room."

I averted my eyes from his face, and said—

"Miss Ryder is very sad at leaving Oxford."

"I should think so," said he, "the feeling is natural. We have chosen our professions, Frank,—you the gay and the brilliant one, and I the grave and the thoughtful; and our choice is seen in our faces. You look exceedingly well, while I——"

"Look very well for a lawyer," interrupted Francis. "We will see you to-morrow early, Phil."

"I will come to hear the Will read, at the Colonel's desire," said Philip. "I feel more gratitude than I can express in words for his great friendship; tell him this."

"What shall I say to Florian?"

Philip bent his head over his parchments. I read his countenance keenly, but it expressed nothing. I observed, however, that his brow knitted and became dark.

"Say nothing," replied he. "I will see her to-morrow."

"Remember, do not write the news to the Major," said Francis, "for I'll take a run down to Oxford myself to tell him."

We returned to Blank Street. In the dusk, I had occasion to go into the library. There was no lamp lighted in the room, only one broad gleam of firelight on the hearthrug. Something stirred in a dark corner. I watched till I saw the gleam of a face and the shadow of a head, then I went near the fire and spoke.

"Who is there?" said I. "It is very dark."

"It is I, Mark!" cried a boyish voice; and Florian's youngest brother limped over and stood beside me.

"What were you doing in this darkness, Master Mark?" said I. "It is not very pleasant to be alone in the dark."

"Yes, it is," replied he, sharply. "I spend hours and hours alone in the dark, when Florian lets me—I like it."

"And how do you spend these long dark hours?" inquired I.

"I read," replied he. "I was reading before you came in."

"What! in darkness and without a book?" exclaimed I, sitting down beside him. Two dark shining eyes looked up to my face through the firelight. He pointed to several books at his feet.

"Don't you see these?" said he. "I had the trouble of climbing up these ladders for them, and they are not the kind of books I care for after all."

"What description of reading do you like?" said I.

"None in particular," answered he. "I sometimes like to read one kind of book, and sometimes another."

"And to what branch of literature do your inclinations now point?"

"To none at all when you are here to speak to," said he. "Are you the tutor, Mr. Gessler, that Florian spoke about?"

"Yes," answered I, flushing. "How did you know I was he?"

"I don't know," said he. "Why are you in this house, Mr. Gessler?"

"Because I am the tutor, Master Mark," replied I.

"Had you many pupils?" inquired he.

"I had one, but I fear I am going to lose him now," said I.

"And whom will you teach now?" asked he.

"I scarcely know yet," replied I. He thought for a moment.

"What did you teach your scholar, Mr. Gessler?"

"I could teach him many things; but he only desired Greek."

"Was he a little boy like me? or perhaps you would not teach little boys, would you?"

"My last pupil was a grown man," said I, "but a bad scholar, because he would not learn. I should like to teach good little boys, who were fond of learning."

"I am very fond of learning," said he, quickly. "Will you teach me? I broke my leg you know; or at least some nasty nurse I had broke it for me. I was too lame and ill to go out to school, for I had to be driven in a wheeled chair from room to room, and out into the garden. Florian and Philip used to read to me pretty stories, but they never taught me anything. Will you teach me, Mr. Gessler?"

"With the greatest delight," answered I. He laughed heartily, as if greatly pleased, and clapped his hands merrily.

"Papa and Florian were always speaking of getting a tutor for me at home. They made it a great grave matter of business; but I have engaged one myself. How surprised they will be!"

"But will they be satisfied?" questioned I.

"Oh! Florian will!"

"It is time for us to see each other," said I, lighting a lamp.

"I'm not a pretty boy," said he. Nobody says I'm pretty but Florian," and he seemed to hide himself from the light.

There was no deformity, save that one shoulder was raised above the other; but the formation of the head and face showed that the defect was not organic, but the result of accident. The countenance was small and round, and the features soft and childlike; the complexion was generally pallid and wan with ill health; but now, when excitement, and the warm light of the fire and the lamp shone upon it, the tints had the pale richness of a fine old picture. The large black eyes had a languid expression, and the hair (a dark chesnut) hung in short locks all round his head. The face was exceedingly expressive, too much so indeed at times, for it revealed too quickly and vividly the sharp pain from which he suffered so frequently. I cannot give a sketch of his character, for no one could read or fathom it. Certain traits and peculiarities, too rare to be familiar, rendered it obscure. He would have perplexed the metaphysician as much as Hamlet.

"I think you are pretty enough, Master Mark," said I, "if you were more ruddy and robust, which I trust you will soon be."

"No, I won't!" cried he, sharply and bitterly; "I'll never be red and strong; I can't go playing, and racing, and bird-nesting, like other boys (oh! how I wish I could), and I'll always be this way. The doctors and Florian say I shall get better, and not be lame soon, but I don't believe them."

"You do not believe them," echoed I; "for shame, Mark."

"No, I don't, Mr. Gessler!" cried he, decidedly; "they once made a nasty pill, and rolled it up in sugar; I ate it, paugh! but it did not do me any good, and I never took a pill again."

Soft footsteps sounded without. I stood rapt and listening, holding my very breath to hear them. They were Florian's,—she came to the door.

"Oh! Marrie, Marrie!" cried she, "I knew I should find you among the books."

Then she observed me, and a blush like the deepening tints of a moss rose diffused itself over her face.

"Florian, Florian!" shouted Mark, "I've found a tutor at last, and he has consented to teach me. I won't have any other schoolmaster, Florian, I tell you that. Speak to her, Mr. Gessler, and tell her that you'll come."

"I am powerless, Miss Ryder," said I, helplessly.

"I understand," answered Florian. "Mark is very wilful."

We grew silent with the serious embarrassment of the position, but we could not help ourselves; we were thrown together by destiny; others made our fates, and not ourselves. If we had I would have fled from Florian, and she from me; we knew the danger of being together, and that instant separation would have been safe and honourable.

"What if I should find a better tutor for you?" said I. "I am not gay, cheerful, and light-hearted, Master Mark; I should only be the grave, dull schoolmaster, and nothing more."

"I don't care," cried Mark, "I should like *you* better."

"Perhaps I cannot come," exclaimed I; "I think I cannot."

Mark began to weep passionately.

"After you promised," he exclaimed, amid his tears; "after you said you would be glad to come. You are a cruel, hard-hearted man, have made my head ache, and my heart beat. I—I—"

Florian's eyes met mine again; there was a question in her glance, and an answer in mine.

I bowed my head.

"Hush, hush! dearest Marrie," said she, and her voice was like the coo of a ring-dove. "Mr. Gessler is to come; hush, hush!"

CHAPTER VII.

THE WILL.—A LAST LETTER.—FLORIAN IN PERPLEXITY.—THE VISITORS DEPART.

"A trouble weighed upon her."—*Tennyson.*

MARK, the little rascal, after he had gained his purpose, grew quite caressing; throwing his arms around his sister's neck, he said—

"You are a dear good girl, Florian, give me a kiss. I feel quite breathless and weary; I wish I had not climbed those ladders for these nasty books."

And he went nearer to Florian, and she crept closer to him, as if they would not even let a shadow come between them.

"Remember, I obey you in remaining, Miss Ryder," said I.

"I have no doubt on that point," answered Florian, quietly. "Were it not so, I would not desire you to be Mark's teacher. You will teach him kindly, Mr. Gessler, good lessons, that will grow into habits, and fit him for the duties of life. Come away, Marrie, love."

Madame Mellitton at this moment thrust her head in at the library door, and abruptly drew back again.

"I shall do my utmost for Mark," replied I, "both by precept and example."

At parting she offered me her hand, and the touch of it was my guerdon.

That evening Selim presented me with a letter; as the address was written in a strange female handwriting, I inquired from whom he had received it. He answered with ineffable archness—

"From a lady, sir."

"From a lady," echoed I, in amazement. "There must be some mistake here, Selim; I know no lady but—but——"

Protesting that it could not be for me, I opened the letter.

"My dear sir," it ran, "come to my chamber to-morrow after the reading of the Will; I will expect you to remember correctly all the particulars of it, or at least its substance. Your doing so may benefit you as much, if not more, than it will benefit me. We do not know what ties may exist between ourselves and strangers. I wish you would bear this in your memory always. I am my second name still; pray satisfy no one's curiosity regarding me. MERCIA MELLITTON."

"Any answer, sir?" said Selim. "I do hopes there is, sir."

"Tell Madame Millitton that I will do as she desires," said I.

Next morning was that destined for the reading of the Will. At the appointed hour Mr. Leer arrived, followed by a small boy bearing a blue bag. As he paused on the threshold, the Coloned advanced towards him, and bowing said—

"Mr. Deer, I presume; the legal gentleman who had the kindness to write me?"

Mr. Leer did not seem quite pleased at the liberty taken with his name, and after correcting the Colonel's mistake, the latter continued—

"I beg a thousand pardons! pray excuse my defective memory! Mr. Leer, I am delighted to see you. Mr. Tamper and Marr will come, I trust."

"Make no apology, Colonel," said Mr. Leer, mildly, in the manner of a priest who granted absolution. "I need not say how happy I am at this auspicious (I mean melancholy) meeting. Our friends will assuredly be here at the hour. What time is it now?"

"Half-twelve, sir," put in his apparently glib and nimble assistant.

His master frowned him down.

"I have brought the Will, Colonel Ryder," continued the lawyer.

"They surely remain away beyond the appointed time," exclaimed the heir.

"Here they are, Colonel," said Mr. Leer, donning his glasses.

Soon after Mr. Tamper and Philip Marr

entered, and the different members of the household began to assemble.

"Where is your sister, Mark?" said the Colonel. "Why is she not here?"

"I left her crying in her own room, papa," said Mark, "and she said she would come as soon as she was able to feel composed."

Still Florian did not appear, although all the others were present.

"Does she look very wretched and unhappy?" exclaimed Philip to me. "I fear yet long to see her; she may meet me with an appearance of love; pity and gratitude may force her to speak softly to me; or she may be the heiress, and in her pride may grudge me a look! Answer me, Gessler, you saw her."

"She indeed seems exceedingly miserable," said I.

This was a cruel reply to his question, increasing his pain, suspense, and doubt, as I *intended* it should.

Passion rose above honour; and I desired to widen the gulf of suspicion that yawned between Florian and my rival.

"Then she is unhappy?" said he. "She

regards herself as a sacrifice. Your words would imply this."

I was silent, and during that silence Florian came in. She was attired in a flowing black dress. Her hair was plainly folded around her head. She was without ornament of any kind save one small gem, a gift of Philip's, that glittered on her hand. Her face was colourless, and her large blue eyes were full and sad with tears. She gazed round the chamber, and a cloud gradually spread itself over her gentle face, and when her glance rested on Philip and me, the melancholy by which she was oppressed became clearly legible in the expression of her countenance.

The Colonel presented Messrs. Tamper and Leer to her. She bowed to them and then to us, and afterwards sat down beside Mark.

"She did not even give me her hand," muttered Philip; "but welcomed me as if I were one of her father's lawyers."

"Have some consideration," said I, impatiently. "Remember the occasion, and see how melancholy and downcast she appears."

Mr. Leer, with the Will in his hand, then

seated himself with as much solemnity as if his chair were a pulpit, and broke the seals—

"The reason," he said, "why the Will of our dear deceased friend, our mutual friend, Mr. Albert Beranger, will be read (contrary to established custom), prior to the interment of his body, will be explained in this letter from our deceased friend to his nearest living relation, his cousin, Colonel Edmund Ryder, which, conforming to the wishes of our deceased friend, I will now proceed to read:—

"DEAR RYDER,

"The last letter I wrote you was from Rome. I did not write you then to forgive you; I was young and hasty at that time, and in my anger wrote bitter things. But a lifetime has passed since that day, and I am almost old now, and from my deathbed I pen you a calm letter, to say that I forgive you (I need not say for what, I think you remember it). The import of my Will shows how much I have forgiven all, and to-morrow I shall have forgotten it for ever. Therefore, let us now wipe out this offence—half folly and half crime—of a lifetime, which has sown hatred and estrangement between us for twenty-two years. It is my part as a dying man to forgive it, and yours to live and forget it. I love Baptist too well to make him rich; wealth is the curse of genius, and gnaws it with a golden tooth. His aims and wishes are beyond its reach, it can purchase nothing that he dreams of or values; therefore, I leave him as he is. I would be buried within sight of my dear birthplace, on the shores of that glorious sea which murmured as my cradle rocked beside it; my body is therefore to be embalmed by my countryman, Mustapha, who will afterwards bear me to my country—my home—and my grave! He will perform this operation where he thinks fit: and it is my injunction that his actions be not interfered with. Let all who ever felt one emotion of regard for me, look at me once more, ere I go across the dark sea to my sunny grave beyond it; let them come that my spirit may see how many or how few really loved me. I will not bless you, I have done that already, having left you my blessing of—gold!

"I am faint, sick, and weary of life, and in my prayer for mercy I cry for rest. Waiting then for the time when the 'dead shall live' and man shall rise in immortality, I lie down, thine till the Resurrection,

"ALBERT BERANGER."

After the reading of this letter, not a word or even a whisper was heard from any one; all sat speechless; the Colonel blanched, Baptist grew flushed, and Mustapha stroked his beard and smiled. But the silence was broken by Pietro Wells, who cried joyfully,—

"Albert forgave him! Albert forgave him! think of that!"

Florian took away her hand and handkerchief from her face; it was pale, and her expression indicated suffering; her eye wandered from countenance to countenance, till it rested on her father's. He avoided her glance, and gazed at the usher, as if he could have shot him. Then came the Will. If a Will were not a legal document, and if lawyers were not the authors of it, what a brief composition it would be! But law, so prodigal of barbarous words and tangled sentences, had found it necessary to express the final Will of the deceased at great length. Colonel Ryder was left heir to all Mr. Beranger's fortune, which was immense; consisting of great landed property in Constantinople and other parts of Turkey, and in large sums of money lodged in foreign and English banks. Baptist had a life annuity of four hundred pounds, with the use of apartments in all Mr. Beranger's houses, subject to the guardianship of the Colonel. Madame Muscat was also left an annuity of fifty pounds. It was Mr. Beranger's desire that none of his domestics should be dismissed. Pietro Wells was endowed with some books.

"How kind of him!" cried the usher, in an ecstasy of gratitude. These books are worth hours of life, I'd even buy them with years of existence; one of them holds the remaining fragments of Tyrtæus, Mr. Gessler!"

When I pictured the wretched chamber, with its sputtering rushlight, wherein he was destined to enjoy the books, I thought a little bitterly of the uselessness of the legacy. As for myself, I was thus mentioned,—

"I engaged Mr. Gerald Gessler for one year, to be tutor and companion to Baptist. It now rests with themselves to cancel or ratify the agreement at will. If they decide upon the former course, give Mr. Gessler his stipulated salary, and the statuette of Janus which he admired so much, as a memento of me."

With these words the Will ended. Baptist started up, and, apparently in a state of great excitement, approached Mr. Leer.

"Is there nothing else?" cried he, in an angry voice. "Have you read it all to the last word? Does he say no more about me than that? Are there no letters, no codicil, no scrap or atom of paper?"

"None," replied Mr. Leer, shrinking back. "I never missed a word in a process during my existence, and, with Heaven's help, I never shall. The instrument is perfect, there is not a flaw in it; examine it yourself."

"No—no—no!" exclaimed Baptist, impatiently, pushing the paper away; "I have heard enough. How bitter it is for one to despise the dead as much as he must the living!" His glance round the room made this compliment a general one. The Colonel swelled with indignation.

"Your words and behaviour at such a time are indecorous, sir," cried he. "It is unbecoming a gentleman or a man to display a mercenary feeling of disappointment so openly and rudely. My daughter is in this room, sir, and in using such expressions you have insulted her."

"No, papa," said Florian, in a low voice, "he has not insulted me; he meant no insult to anyone!"

"Miss Ryder!" frowned her father, "you speak strangely."

"I am satisfied that you understand my meaning," said Baptist to Florian; "*you* could not do otherwise; you are not one to find base motives in men's common words. What I have to say to you, Colonel Ryder, I shall say to you alone on some other occasion."

"What is your name, sir?" said the Colonel, pompously; "I confess that I am not quite sure of it."

"My name!" echoed Baptist, knitting his crimson brow; "we must speak of *that*, too, when we meet." He bowed to Florian, and then left the chamber, followed by every eye, the Colonel looking at him with a sneer as he went out.

"We must excuse him," said he, "even although we despise him; he has lost a fortune. Gentlemen, allow me to thank you for your kindness on this ausp—— hem! sad occasion."

"Masters!" said Dr. Mustapha, rising, "as I leave this house with my friend Beranger very shortly, I will be glad to see you all in his bedroom in a few minutes. Bismillah! he wanted to bid you all farewell quietly, and I hope you will come, this priest and all."

"Sir," replied Mr. Leer, smiling softly, "I am no priest."

"We will all come, Doctor," said Colonel Ryder.

Mustapha disappeared, his face wearing a common expression. When he left, Florian drew her father into a window, her countenance darkening even in the sunlight. Laying her hands on his arm, and looking him in the face, she said,—

"Papa, what had Mr. Beranger to forgive? What did you ever do, father, in all your life that needed this great forgiveness?"

He gave a forced laugh.

"Pooh, pooh!" answered he; "what a ridiculous minx you are, Florian! Do you expect me to recollect all the foolish quarrels I have had, when I was a young rascal, with the young fellows I used to meet at college and at quarters? I have been a mad undergraduate and a gay ensign in my time, Florian, you know. Besides, had I done Beranger any wrong, is it natural to think that he would have forgiven me and left me his heir? Pooh! you are a silly little bird!"

"Oh! papa, don't say that," cried Florian, a tear sparkling on her cheek. "We never feel perfectly happy till we have forgiven something—never quite miserable till we have done some ill which it is hard for another to forgive. Oh! papa, forgiveness is as blessed and easy as love!"

"Don't preach, Florian," said the Colonel, who was in high humour at finding himself rich. "Billing and cooing become you better; go and speak to Phil."

He hastened after the usher and caught him by the arm. Pietro Wells turned, and when he saw who touched him, his face changed. An unusual fire glowed on his features, his torpid feelings were evidently excited, for he was in a rage!

"I shake ye off," cried he, through his teeth. "Your hand is heavy on me; as heavy on me now as it was then. You are the same dog that I kicked on the streets of Constantinople. You are Edmund Ryder. I shake you off!"

"This is absurd, my dear sir," said the Colonel. "Books have muddled your brain. If you dared to kick me on the streets of Constantinople (a circumstance which I forget, however), I feel assured that I returned you the favour on the spot, therefore, it does not much matter. I came after you to have a chat on college days, and to speak about old friends, now far away or dead."

"What we truly love is never dead," answered the usher, forcibly. "You may fling away your cobweb loves like a handful of dust; but you cannot tear down the old noble watch-dog of the ruin and the grave—the brave green ivy! You cannot make me think my friends dead, or forget *him*. Don't look at me; I hate you."

He laid his hands on my arm to hurry me on, and the bony, trembling fingers seemed to cut through the flesh like teeth. The Colonel, with a short laugh, went away. When I returned to the library I searched eagerly for Florian. She sat by a reading desk, and her hand worked nervously with the leaves of a book, while the sunlight caught the brilliant on her finger, which flashed and glittered with every movement. I did not see her face, for it was turned towards the window. Philip was standing by her chair speaking to her; his face was hidden also. Stung with restless and inquisitive jealousy, I approached them, to become a spy and an eavesdropper if I could, for I burned to know how she had met him, and what she was saying to him. I did not muffle my footsteps, but they were too much engrossed and agitated to hear me.

"I cannot speak about this matter now, Mr. Marr," said she; "but it is my earnest desire to do so, at some other time."

"Have you anything new to say on the subject, Florian?" returned Philip, with some bitterness. "You are wealthy now, and I am poor; and your manner shows that you have something to say on our marriage, that you never said before."

"Perhaps I have," exclaimed Florian. "Perhaps I am the slave and tool of something that you know nothing about. But let me ask you this question; was my demeanour to you ever different from what it is at this moment?"

"Yes," answered Philip, "not warmer, perhaps, but different. A shadow lay between us before, now it seems to be a substance. Whether you loved me or not in Oxford, I felt you to be mine, wholly and entirely; but now, whether you love me or not, I feel that you are no longer mine. I have a presentiment that our union can never be accomplished. I feel as if something were drawing you away from me, Florian, not from my heart, but my arms. It is a strange thought; but even while you are at my side, I feel as if you were lost!"

He took her small hand, and the glitter of the brilliant was extinguished. I moved, and he let it fall. The sunlight glittered on the jewel again. A singular rapture filled my heart, for I learned from these few words what course Florian meant to pursue. It was evident that she intended to beg or take her freedom from Philip; and why?—for whom? A selfish hope glowed in the depths of my soul. Oh! that she desired liberty for my sake! Philip's sacrifices and struggles for her, their long engagement, and his intense affection for his affianced bride, became as nothing to me; passion was rampant. I reasoned falsely with myself. He could not love her more absorbingly than I did; he could exist as well without her as I. I had as little right as he to submit tamely to that blank existence which must be mine if fate condemned me to live eternally without her. My love could count its long years as well as his. Had not her eyes declared to me the passion of her heart more eloquently than any words her tongue had ever spoken to him? I sat down in a large reading-chair, and their voices again reached me.

"Florian!" said Philip, gravely, "in speaking to you now, I will give up the hackneyed habit of love-making; let us look upon it for a few minutes as a matter of business—a law process, if you like. Years ago, in Oxford, with the consent of our parents, we became betrothed to each other, and you were willing to be my wife. Years passed, and you were still willing. As my future wife you met me, spoke to me, wrote to me; and in all the years of our betrothal you never raised a protest against the engagement. A certain date was fixed for our marriage—(it is at this hour only two months distant!)—preparations have been making for it, friends talked of the approaching nuptials, and you talked of them to friends. In the meantime you become rich; and the new-found wealth is only barely yours, when you tell me—if not distinctly in words, at least by your manner—that you will not now be my wife."

"That I *cannot*, you mean," interrupted Florian, in a low voice.

"I see no difference between the two modes of expression," said Philip, "as they mean the same thing—you are not to be my wife. But let me still continue to treat it as a matter of business and law; I have your oral promise, and your written declaration, to be my wife. And I now ask you to fulfil the promise, or to tell me plainly and truthfully why you will *not*. Whether you love me or not," he continued, "is not the question at issue. If the plea of not loving me exists now, it must have existed at the time of our engagement; and as it was not mentioned then as a barrier, it ought not to be mentioned as a barrier now. If you urge this plea, I will not accept it; it would be folly, and not justice, to do so. Perhaps you have formed some attachment; perhaps it is the old trick of being off with the old love before being on with the new. But I will not consider that plea as admissible either. Justice demands that you should only be my wife. I will never abandon my claim on you; I will not be the victim, neither will I let you be the victim, of a caprice or a folly; if you are fickle and whimsical, I will not let your fickleness and whimsicality injure yourself or me. Do you comprehend what I have said, Florian? and what inference do you draw from it?"

There was a moment's silence, and my heart beat loudly; for my fate, as well as Philip's, hung upon her reply.

"What inference do you draw, Florian?" repeated Philip.

"That you will show me no mercy in my bitter trial," said she.

"What mercy do you seek, Florian?" said he.

"Freedom!" she exclaimed, clasping her hands like a captive or a slave.

"And what will you do with it?" asked he, bitterly. "Marry, and give it to another, I suppose? No! that mercy to you would be none to myself. My heart is suffering unendurable pangs in consequence of your fickleness. No, Florian, it is impossible; you pray in vain to me; I cannot give you up."

"You will not give me up?" cried she; "say it again."

"I will say it a thousand times!" exclaimed he; "while I am a man I'll say it; while I live I'll say it! I have strong passions. I have accustomed myself to sweet, delicious dreams, which you alone can realize. The love which I feel for you is not only a passion, but a long, inveterate habit, which I cannot throw away or live without. I tell you, Florian Ryder, that you must be my wife. I do not coerce you, I but keep you to a promise. You dare not break this vow of yours, for my heart is bound to it, and you will trample on both in trampling on one. You dare not."

"What if I am forced to dare it?" exclaimed she.

"Have you no mercy, no compassion, no remembrance?" cried Philip. "Do you forget Oxford days?—our lonely saunters through the woods, our walks in the little garden?—my ravings, my hopes about you and the future?—

the fame which I was to acquire and you to share, and the home we were to enjoy together? Have you the heart and sympathies of a human being, and yet do you forget all this, and even almost reproach me for not forgetting it also?"

"Oh! what if I must?" sobbed she. "Do you think I forget my kind brother, Philip, at Oxford? Do you think I would pain him or forsake him if I could? But, Philip, you do not know what power impels me to this step. It is stronger than gratitude, friendship, memory, or sympathy, and I must yield to it, God help me, and to none other! Philip, do not look so cruelly resolute; give me up, oh! pray do. I will soon be a pale, wasted, miserable thing, that you could not love if you would."

"Let me ask you a question?" said Philip. "Am I right in concluding that the power which impels you is love—love for another? Now if that is your plea, it goes for nothing with me. I cannot yield to your desire. But what did your last words mean? are you ill?"

"Yes, very ill," answered Florian. "A weary, restless, feverish agony, a wistful looking after something, I know not what, that I may never discover, a heart-consuming outlooking, a wasting sickness of the soul and mind, heart and brain, seizes me in the night-time; it seems like the coming on of death, and in the darkness I pray to be allowed to die when it is light."

"Get physicians, child, and follow their advice," said Philip.

"I had one physician," answered she; "and what he said made me think it useless to call in another. I shall soon part with the misery of my own existence. Oh! be generous, Philip, and give me up."

"The Colonel urged our marriage in Oxford," said Philip; "and he urges it now. He has set his heart upon the union. Does he know of or approve this change?"

"I am afraid to tell him, Philip," said Florian. "My heart is breaking with the fear and anxiety. I should like to die to-night, before the anger and distrust of all fall upon me to-morrow. I hope and pray that I may never see another summer falling sweetly over the earth. Love again, Philip, and do not ask me from my father; remember Oxford, and have pity on me!"

There was a pause. Much though I loved Florian, had that appeal been uttered to me, I would have yielded her up. I listened anxiously; perhaps the prayer was breathed for me.

"Do you not remember, Florian, that we never forget?" said Philip. "Do you not know that man and woman know no second love? that first love is life's love? I cannot love another; this passion can never be extinguished, not even when I am aged and grey. Love is the sweet necessity of man's life, of toil and ambition. My decision is taken."

"What is it?" cried Florian, wildly. "Oh! be merciful!"

"I am merciful, Florian," said he. "I will not give you up."

"Yes, you are merciful to yourself, and not to me!" exclaimed she. "You are egotistical—selfish—severe; a man who loved me for myself, and not for what is mine, would have given me up!"

"No, he would not!" cried Philip, warmly. "No true man would; a fool or a coward might. Rob a brave man, and he will strike the robber down and defend his property; but rob a coward, and he will abandon all and run away. I was not mercenary in Oxford, and you know I am not mercenary now. Florian Ryder, at the time first appointed I will come to claim you as my wife."

"Very well, come!" returned she, in a strange, hard voice.

"And in the meantime," said he, "there must be no coquetries or sentimental friendships with young gentlemen. Nature has made me jealous, and I will be a frightful rival when you call my jealousy forth. Before I leave this spot, our positions must be settled; you are to conduct yourself on all occasions as an affianced bride—as *my* bride."

"As your slave!" said Florian, proudly. "But I will not be your slave, sir. I will make friendships with whom I choose. My decision also is taken."

"We must not part thus," said Philip; "the desperation and frenzy of my love must not be regarded as tyranny and suspicion; there is no slavery in the idea of wife."

Their interview was interrupted by the entrance of Dr. Mustapha, who came to summon us to the bedroom.

"Take my arm, Florian," said Philip, "and lean on me."

She hung back, but he drew her hand through his arm, and they walked from the room. I followed them.

The coffin had been removed from the bedroom into a small lofty apartment hung with black cloth. It was broad day, but the light was carefully excluded, and wax candles in gold candlesticks burned beside the bier. The physician stood at the head of the coffin, solemn and majestic, without a muscle moving in his face, which was as calm and rigid as that of a statue. As we entered he raised the cerement from the face of the corpse, that we might gaze for the last time at Mr. Beranger.

Although so composed and motionless,

there was still such an appearance of life in the features of the deceased, that we should not have been surprised if, like one awaking from a profound sleep, he had suddenly risen and addressed us.

"It is a pity that the dead cannot speak," said Baptist.

"It is sometimes as difficult to make the quick," said Dr. Mustapha. "I am afraid all my art and precious waters and ointments will not make him look better than this. Stand a little to the left, Colonel."

Pietro Wells, who stood silently by the bier, drenching the shroud with tears, now wrung his hands, and uttered a cry of anguish.

"Oh! that he could speak! Oh! that he could speak!" cried he. "Do you yet live, Albert, in any other sphere? Oh! that he could break this silence of death, speak to me, and resolve my doubts. You know all about it now, you have seen everything or nothing; you have found the chaos, or the world beyond. Oh! dear Albert, speak!"

Dr. Mustapha hastily covered the face, and

Florian, who was deadly pale with some strong emotion, turned away with a shudder and a groan; she withdrew her hand from Philip's arm, and taking that of her father she left the room.

"That will be Florian's course through life," said Philip to me, sadly and bitterly; "in sickness and sorrow, when she is ill, and weak, and weary, she will turn from me and seek some other support. She is a strange being; I must have mistaken her character. Oh! that she would interpret herself!"

"Circumstances change feelings," said I, averting my face. "She will explain her conduct satisfactorily yet, or events will. Be patient, Marr, you cannot understand a woman in a moment."

He smiled, and we walked into the drawing-room.

"Do you know what I thought Mr. Beranger looked like?" said Mr. Leer to Mr. Tamper.

"A mummy," suggested his friend.

"No," replied Mr. Leer, with a solemn shake of the head.

"Wax-work," said Mr. Tamper; "I thought he resembled a well-moulded and painted wax-work."

"No," returned Mr. Leer, in a voice tremulous with deep feeling, as if there was something touching in the idea of "wax-work."

"What the deuce did he look like, then?" exclaimed Mr. Tamper, impatiently; "present your new idea to the minds of your audience."

"Life!" said Mr. Leer, awfully. "When the cloth was raised, I said to myself, 'It may strike no other person in the room in the same manner, but *I* think it resembles life.'"

I felt the soft touch of a glove on my arm, and turned round.

"How do you do, Mr. Gessler?" said Mr. Tamper; "glad to see you. We have seen the last of poor Beranger."

"I am sorry that we have," said I. "I have lost a kind and generous master in Mr. Beranger."

"There are plenty more of kind friends in the world," said Mr. Tamper; "and a great number of generous masters. That's right, Marr, look after Miss Ryder."

"I was not conscious of looking after her," said Philip.

"Don't say a word against the indictment," returned Mr. Tamper, "for there's not a pleasanter thing in life (after business hours) than to admire and love the women. Hard-working men, like us lawyers, could not live without them for a day; the very presence of a bonnet in Court acts on us like a pint of Castalia taken at a draught. We don't think them heavenly, as other men swear false oaths they do; because, between you and me, a lawyer could not by any means appreciate anything better than a woman—he could not enjoy an angel! There, I must plead guilty, it is a way of mine; and I do believe that if candour were even a hanging matter I'd be candid to the last swing. Bless the dear women! I confess to present bachelorism with an invisible blush, but I can look humanity in the face, for I want to—to marry, and have wanted to marry for the last twenty years; and, believe me, there's glory in the very intention, and virtue in the bare wish!"

"Better for some, perhaps, that they

never loved, or desired to marry," said Philip.

"Pooh! pooh! pooh!" exclaimed Mr. Tamper. "Here is a wretched man, Mr. Gessler, who actually wants to be a bachelor! By-the-bye, Mr. Gessler, do you mean to reside in London?"

I answered in the affirmative.

"Very well," continued he; "you will receive a communication from me very shortly, I have no time to enter into particulars just now. But, recollect, keep yourself disengaged till you hear from me."

I found Madame Mellitton in travelling dress when I sought her after the reading of the Will.

"I was awaiting you," said she, stiffly. "I must be out of this house in a quarter of an hour. I feared I should be too late for the train."

"Do you go to Oxford?" said I.

She bowed.

"Perhaps I shall have occasion to go there soon myself," said I.

"Remember that you will not breathe to Dr. Castellon or my daughter that you have seen me here!" exclaimed she. "Who is the heir? I listened outside the door, but the lawyer spoke so indistinctly that I could not hear."

"Colonel Ryder," answered I. She gasped with surprise.

"Edmund Ryder Albert Beranger's heir!" her voice and manner expressing the greatest amazement and terror of which a human voice is capable. She sat down, and tore a glove to pieces.

"You appear surprised," said I; "the Colonel was Mr. Beranger's cousin, you know."

"And his enemy and mine!" said she, in her deep, hard, dry tones. "He is dead, but, let him go to any paradise he pleases, my curse will follow him! Were you and Baptist in the Will also?"

I told her in what terms we were mentioned.

"How did he look when you saw him last?" said she.

"Calm, happy, triumphant, and life-like," replied I.

Madame Mellitton sprung up.

"But he is not calm, and happy, and triumphant," hissed she, fiercely; "he is tortured—restless—damned! He deceived you all; he was a wretched hypocrite even till the day of his death. He is in misery, I tell you eternal misery. Now, I must go." She threw some wrappers over her arm, and took a reticule into her hand; then she addressed me again.

"I saw a girl in the library with you last night, and a little boy; were they Ryders?"

"Yes," replied I; "Miss Florian and Mark; the Colonel's eldest and only daughter and his second son."

"Was that creature—was she like her mother?" asked Madame Mellitton.

"I never saw the late Mrs. Ryder," said I; "but I believe her daughter resembles her very much."

"Indeed," said she, "and in character also?"

"Yes," said I, "her brother told me so."

"And is the character good and noble?" inquired she.

"Exceedingly so," replied I; "her reputation for benevolence, amiability, and gentleness is well known in Oxford."

"Ah! when you come to Oxford, call on us; and now farewell. I can never acquire the habit of your hand-shaking at meeting and parting; so excuse me!"

And Madame, with a stiff formal courtesy, departed. With all her singularity of mien and manner she did not strike me as being eccentric. There was so much thought and firm purpose on her countenance, that one could not think so for a moment.

The day wore on quietly till evening came; then we heard the dull terrible footsteps of the coffin-bearers as they descended the stairs, and went out to the black-blinded coach, where Mustapha sat waiting. The lamps flickered on the gilded velvet, the heavy tassels swung like tongueless bells in the air. The domestics were weeping on the threshold, and the idle boys without stood and gazed on the funeral pomp. The coach moved away, and Mr. Beranger was gone for ever. I leaned on the banisters sadly, with feelings of natural sorrow and regret. Selim touched me.

"Massy! sir," said he. "It's away now for ever from this here 'ouse, and I'm happy for to see that the black 'un (the gallipot which is a heathen you know, sir), has follered it to the end! Do you know what I sawed, sir?"

"I have not the least idea, Selim" said I.

"Joe, if you please, sir," said he, "for lookee, sir, I'm back to my old toggery of green and silver; when the Colonel sawed me, he got tall and mighty like. 'Boy,' says he, 'go and take off that maskerade!' But as I was going to tell you, sir, when Madame Mellitton left this here 'ouse, I was just a-going to see the old 'uns at 'ome, (for I did not see my father which was sick for a month), and bless you, sir, people a-does have feelins, whether they are dressed like heathens or not,—I saw Madame Mellitton a-going into a small 'otel round the corner; and she drew down the blind on the front winder, and sat staring out, a-watching of this here 'ouse, sir: and when the black coach went away, she got into a cab and told cabby to foller it. She's a deep 'un, sir; she told Madame Muscat that she had not a minute to spare, as she was going by the train, and there was she all day in that there 'otel!"

This news was very perplexing to me; what close connection had the Castellons, with Mr. Beranger and the Ryders? There seemed no chance of my discovering this.

Pietro Wells took to his beloved books again; and had just settled himself comfortably to a work entitled the "Polity of the Lacedemonians," chuckling over the anticipated literary feast, when the door burst open, and Baptist, flushed and hasty, went straight up to him. The usher stared vacantly at him.

"You knew him well," cried Baptist, vehemently. "You were schoolfellows together; you knew him from his boyhood! Do not deny it."

Pietro Wells glanced appealingly to me, and began to read.

"Mr. Wells does not know to whom you allude," said I.

"The dead man; Mr Beranger!" said Baptist, impetuously. "You knew him? speak!"

"I don't know if I knew him," said the usher, reflectively, laying down his book. "I don't know if I *knew* him, but I loved him very much: poor Albert!"

"Had he a brother?" said Baptist, calmly, his dim eyes glancing for a moment as if with the kindling of a hope. "Had he a brother?"

"No!" answered the usher, his eyes still buried in his book. "No; he had no brother."

"Had he a sister?" inquired Baptist, again, becoming calmer at every question.

"No!" replied Pietro Wells, with a sigh. Nor a sister: I wish I had never had one either."

"Then, sir," said Baptist, still, in the midst of all his excitement, preserving his self-possession, "Then, sir—you who are his old schoolfellow and old friend—who am I?"

"His nephew!" replied the usher, with brief simplicity.

Baptist laughed scornfully.

"Ay! it were logical and natural to suppose so," said he, in mocking tones. "Very probable, indeed, that I should be the nephew of a man who never had brother or sister—very probable!"

Baptist, seeing how difficult it was to fix

Pietro Wells's mind on questions the purpose of which he did not comprehend, shook him again, and cried,—

"Awake—awake! Who am I? Speak!"

"How should I know?" replied the usher, with a patient wail. "I never saw you before. I cannot call you by name!"

"Listen!" said Baptist, speaking with slow energy. "I shall tell you the story of my life. Hear me, every word!"

CHAPTER VIII.

BAPTIST'S STORY.—FRANCIS AND EAGLE.—FLORIAN'S HOME.—A FAREWELL.

"But then the face, so arch and full of mirth."—*Rogers.*

"ALBERT BERANGER was the first and only remembered being of my childhood. He reared and seemed to love me, with a strange affection that, although not unmingled with pain, never chilled once for nineteen years. He did not send me to college or public schools, but engaged tutors for me at home. These masters instilled into my mind, by lesson and book, the same principles which my guardian taught me in conversation—a hatred and distrust of woman, and an enervating Epicureanism. But I never learned those lessons, I rather despised them; ambition saved me from being a follower of Epicurus, and made me a disciple of Zeno and Aristotle. I resisted many artfully-urged temptations,—wine-drinking, indolence, selfish and sensual indulgence, and opium-smoking. He once prevailed upon me to smoke one of his ivory pipes. I did so, and became lapped in a delicious sensation, that was neither sleep, waking, dreaming, nor madness. He had put opium into the pipe. I broke it, and vowed never to smoke again. But these are small matters, and have no connection with my story. He was a Turk, and deemed all these sensual enjoyments necessities of existence. I blame him not, for he thought and acted as he had been taught.

"I frequently spoke to him about my birth and parentage; and he always told me so earnestly and kindly that he would never die without revealing all about my father and my mother, that I believed him all my life. I used to pray and beseech him to tell me of my mother, anything about *her*, only one simple memory; but he would not, he would always point to the future. And now procrastination has done its accustomed work! Sometimes I doubted his whole story, even my relationship to him; but he vowed sacredly that I was of his blood. He also frequently asserted that I alone should be his heir. Has he not, now, in his coffin, on his way to his grave, proved himself to be a liar—a covenant-breaker—a violator of vows and promises? I never forfeited his affection; I never rebelled against his will; I never disobeyed his commands; till the last his regard for me seemed unchanged; I never heard that he had a cousin or relation alive on earth; Colonel Ryder's very name was that of a stranger to me. And yet he has almost disinherited me, made this man his heir, and died without leaving me the legacy of a word! Is not my life a mysterious riddle? I am a stranger to my own self, to my country, my birth-place, and my home. I do not even know my own name! Tell me, then, old man, who I am; do not say 'nay,' you may have only one year between you and your grave. Tell me, therefore, as if this act of mercy were the deed by which you would save your soul, who am I? Speak!"

"Come here!" replied Pietro Wells. "Come near to me; my eyes are growing dim; come under the light."

He placed his two lank tremulous hands on Baptist's shoulder, and gazed in his face. He was fast falling into his old dreamy manner, which I knew so well by experience; therefore, while he was near enough to hear me, I shook him by the arm.

"Tell him, Mr. Wells, tell him!" exclaimed I.

He answered only by a low mutter in his native tongue, as though he had been wandering long through other scenes than ours—to the eastern home of his boyhood—and then began to gesticulate sadly. Indeed, I have often observed him do so in one of these waking dreams.

"There is only one face which I distinctly remember," began he. "But I left it very, very far away, farther away than Athens is from this. I never saw a countenance with a trait of that one on it; but if your face, or any other face, had resembled it, I should have known you, I must have known all about you. But yours is not like that face, for you are angry, and you don't love me. But there is another face; stay! when did I see it last? Was it twenty years ago, or yesterday?"

"Does mine resemble *that* face then?" said Baptist.

"Not now, not now; when you are going to weep," answered Pietro Wells, regarding him with a frightened look. "Only then when you prayed with flashing, angry eyes."

"Who was this?" cried Baptist, flushing. "I must know. Look at me; I am praying again."

"She was," continued the usher, shaking his head, "a rash, guilty, pitiless woman, who, for the fleeting passion of a cold, proud, heartless man, stained her honour—broke her vow—and sacrificed the love of true hearts, that she knew would break without her. Oh! what a crime is selfishness, what a crime!"

"That was not my mother!" said Baptist,

proudly. "That could not have been *my* mother!"

"Why should she be? How could she be?" cried the usher, sharply, letting Tyrtæus drop on the floor.

"Answer me one other question and I have done," exclaimed Baptist. "You know, and have known all of Mr. Beranger's blood and kin; who, then, do you suppose I am likely to be?"

"Eh? ay! I believe Albert *was* one of the students who had relations," said the usher, his mind running back to the college where he had been young. "I have heard him speak of them; but with the exception of one they were always far away—as distant then as they are now."

"What exception do you mean?" said Baptist.

"Him!" said the usher, between his teeth. "The heir! Did you speak to *him* about this matter? He should know."

He bent eagerly forward, in expectation of a reply.

"Yes, I have inquired of him," said Baptist; "but his replies were like yours—falsehoods. He said he knew nothing."

The short bitter laugh with which he said this expressed utter unbelief.

"Then go to the Will," said the usher, becoming practical. "All his kindred must have been in the Will; Albert would not have left one of them out."

"True," mused Baptist, "that may be true. Old man! this is not all you can tell, but all you will tell; for I know how a man looks when he lies. You may have a feeling of justice and honest gratitude in your heart, and I believe you have; but truth and mercy are as necessary as gratitude. Yet you have not had mercy enough to point me to my mother's grave! Still implacable as you have been to my prayer, I daresay you will pray to-night for yourself."

"Young man," said Pietro Wells, pursuing him to the door, "I have nothing left to pray for; I have never prayed; I will never pray; but I have mercy—mercy for the fly and the worm; mercy above all for man and misery. I have nothing to swear by; but I say to you, and I have never lied, that I do not know who you are. Do you believe me? Come back and say before *him* that you believe me."

Baptist seemed to hesitate, but only for a moment or two.

"Pooh!" said he, "who would revenge himself on an imbecile? I do believe you. Let me pass."

And hurrying past him he went out.

"That is a fierce youth," said the usher, "a fiery-blooded boy. But do you believe my statements?"

"Certainly, Mr. Wells," replied I, "every word of them."

"Do not say more," exclaimed he, quickly. "You believe me, and what do I care for him?"

Pietro Wells never acted the Stoic so severely as he did all that night; for he maintained a rigid fast. He had always abstained from wines; but now he rejected every temptation in the form of the most exquisite dishes that could be offered to him.

I dwelt on Baptist's words—"Tell me of my parents, of my *mother!*" Could I not make an effort also?

When the Colonel heard our intention of going to Oxford, he deputed me to dispose of all their effects in Ivy-nook Cottage; and to give up the house itself to the proprietor.

"You will find it a poor place, Mr. Gessler, a poor place!" said he. "Mrs. Ryder died shortly after our residence there. My eldest son was constantly from home, at college, or with his regiment; my daughter's education was finished in a seminary in London; and, being alone, I saw very little society, and, therefore, did not think it requisite to remodel or furnish the house. You will find it a lumber-house of rubbish."

Pride is a strange thing. The Colonel did not care a rush for me or my opinions, yet he troubled himself to make all these apologies.

"We were all nurtured amid that rubbish, papa," said Florian, reproachfully. "We were happy in that lumber-house; mamma died there. That rubbish held our household gods; and that lumber-house was home! I wish you would not let it. I wish you would let it remain as it is."

"This is a ridiculous rhapsody, Florian,"

said her father, pompously. "In the first place the house is not mine to let, and you would not have me purchase such a place; in the second place, it cannot remain as it is, unless we would commit the absurd extravagance of renting a house which we should never occupy; in the third place, you can have any article you please out of it. I approve of preserving relics which bring the past before us. I, myself, am to commission Mr. Gessler to take away certain things which I shall note down on this card."

Here he gave me a list of articles—a military chest, containing all the articles of a colonel's uniform, a sword which he had wielded at Waterloo, a brace of new mounted pistols, a pair of new Wellington boots, his last hat, a portrait of himself when he was a smart young captain, a miniature of his late wife, and all the portraits of the children I could get. These were the last items on the card, Wellington boots, his last hat, and his new pistols. These were some of the Colonel's relics!

"What I desire will not be so easily carried," said Florian, sighing. "I should not like to mention them to Mr. Gessler, but I will write to Mrs. Stone on the matter; my letter will be in Oxford before yourselves, as I shall write this evening, and she will arrange it all."

"Is it flower-pots?" said the Colonel. "I believe it is. Mr. Gessler, you would not object to carrying some flower-pots here, would you?"

"Not in the least, Colonel," replied I. "I assure you, Miss Ryder, no one would carry them so carefully as I would; you need not fear to entrust them to me."

Florian smiled sadly, and shook her head.

"I loved the flowers you spoke of while I was among them," said she. "But the flowers of one place are as dear to me as the flowers of another; I should not care although I never saw an Oxford flower again."

"You will go to Oxford, then, to-morrow, Mr. Gessler?"

"I'm going too, sir," broke in Francis.

"When you go, Francis," said his father, "call on Dr. Castellon, who resides there, and give him this letter."

"I hope you have introduced me inside," said Francis, "as I never saw the gentleman in my life. I am going purposely to see the old Major, and to tell him the news."

"I am exceedingly glad to hear it," said the Colonel. "I have in my desk a note of invitation written for himself and Miss Eglantine Marr—you will deliver it. The Major is the only remaining Waterloo comrade I have; and as such I value his companionship, and honour himself. And the tie which is yet to unite our families together——"

He gazed at Florian, who hung her head and blushed.

"Putting on uniform at Phil's name, eh, Florian? I'll be away when he comes this evening," cried Francis.

"You had better take Florian away with you, too," said Mark, "for she and Phil are sure to quarrel when they meet, and she will certainly cry when he goes away. He is not half so nice now as he was in Oxford, or so welcome either, I know that."

Florian's face revealed the agitation from which she was now suffering. Her feeling of shame was so acute that she blushed deeply.

The Colonel raised himself and looked black and majestic.

"This boy spoke about engaging you as tutor," said he, "and, by my soul, he gives strong evidence of requiring one. Miss Ryder informed me that you had consented to come, and I trust you will improve the manners in cultivating the mind, for I hold etiquette to be as important as education itself. Now, as to terms?"

"Pray do not mention them," said I, hastily; "they are of no consequence. My chief anxiety is, that I may be able to perform all I desire; but Master Mark looks like a good quick scholar, who will make progress even with an inferior schoolmaster."

"I sincerely hope so," said the Colonel; "the drudgery of study I trust will tame him. But, by the way, what sort of a person is that young man, that artist, whom Mr. Beranger mentioned in his Will? He carried himself very proudly, and addressed me as if I were his equal; what does he imagine himself to be—a genius?"

"It is no imagination," said I, "he is a genius."

"Hem!" exclaimed the Colonel, "it is a difficult matter to find out the possessor of real genius; good pictures are painted, and good books written; they gain a deserved popularity, and yet they are not the works of genius. True genius is generally humble and unassuming, whereas your artist pupil is an arrogant and presuming puppy."

If Baptist had only heard this representation of his character! I have not sought to dwell on the Colonel's own character hitherto, because with all his majesty it was very simple and transparent. Overweening pride, excessive selfishness, and a love of boasting and hectoring, were its conspicuous points. He was proud of his ancestry and rank—of the sounding titles of his forefathers, their matrimonial alliances, wealth, power, and influence; but he did not care a straw whether they were saints or knaves—cowards or brave men; he was not ashamed of their vices or proud of their virtues, the stamp on the gold was all he valued.

His wife had been one of the haughty and beautiful Howards, but she had possessed none of the arrogance and pride which the Colonel thought becoming a person of birth; therefore, if she had not been a Howard, he would have despised her! Florian was his daughter, and the daughter of a Howard, and for this alone he was proud of her; her virtues were nothing to him. He was sorry to see all her mother's imperfections and defects revived in her; the spiritless humility, the quiet tameness of manner, the love of preaching, moralising, and of checking vice and extravagance, an inveterate habit of church-going, and a dislike to parade, display, and society. His chief motives for desiring her to marry Philip Marr, and not a man of more fortune, were that Philip's family was ancient and titled like his own,—his father was an old Waterloo chum,—and when he sanctioned his daughter's betrothal to him their position was so obscure and their finances so low that he had no hopes of obtaining a greater alliance for her. A sense of honour, and a feeling of shame, now prompted him to urge the fulfilment of the engagement, despite their improved fortunes; and his boasted respect for Philip's moral and intellectual worth was all mere hectoring. In his secret heart he regretted the necessity of having to fling away his heiress on a solicitor's clerk. Francis's personal beauty and fascinations were regarded by him with the eye of a huckster; he would sell well, he thought, among heiresses and ladies of rank; for even the *éclat* of birth and wealth gives place humbly to the more brilliant *éclat* of beauty. Mark was stunted in growth, and slightly malformed, he thought; but that was no matter to one of his position and fortunes. Had the Colonel known that I loved his daughter, he would have ordered me away from his house. I discovered afterwards that when the Colonel was in great pecuniary difficulties, brought on by his gambling and betting propensities, Philip had signed certain bills and become security for certain debts of honour, all of which he had to pay in the end; so that he was constrained to feel grateful to his future son-in-law (or at least to feign gratitude), to sustain the honour of an officer and a gentleman.

Perhaps I sketch the Colonel's character too harshly and darkly; but it is not a hasty picture, for it was drawn only after a long and minute study of the man.

I stood once again in the quaint old streets of Oxford, with a thousand bitter feelings throbbing in my heart, all having reference to Florian; my soul was in my love, and hence its bitterness when hope had parted from it. Another man's bride was my idol; these words tell my position, as miserable a one as it was possible for a man to be in. The little cottage of Major Marr stood red and white before us, with a dot of blue in front, for the Major was there, with rake and blue jacket, and Eagle beside him. He ran forward to meet me.

"Mr. Gessler! how do you do?" exclaimed he. "Frank, my boy, I'm glad to see you. How is Florian, and the Colonel, and little Mark, the parson, eh? quite well. Come in, gentlemen; ah! you would rather look at Eagle's runners. Don't you think Eagle has grown, Frank?"

"Beautifully!" answered the Captain, with admiring glances. "Have you been the gardener of all these flowers, Miss Eagle? I feel flattered, for they look quite soldierly in their scarlet jackets; did you mean them as a compliment to the army?"

"No, I didn't!" said Eagle, laughing and blushing. "Papa is the only gardener that ever touches a flower here; and I don't think scarlet a pretty colour for a flower either, it is too glaring and gaudy. I like pale flowers much better, like these convolvuluses and pinks at the gate."

"I'll not have my red-coats scandalized!" cried Francis, plucking a branch of geranium, and putting it among Eagle's lustrous curls. "Look here! Put these in raven hair—on a white bosom—even in small, snowy hands, and how exquisitely they contrast,—the glossy black, the peachy white, and the transparent scarlet!"

Miss Eagle shook the geraniums from her dark curls like a bird flinging chains from its wings.

"Put it in your button-hole, Francis," said the Major, "and say nothing more on the matter; you can never argue a woman down, especially if she's pretty. But, to change the subject, what news have you for us?"

"Wonderful news! glorious news!" cried Francis.

"Speak it out, then!" exclaimed the Major, "and don't hang fire. Are you to be married at last, eh?" The old Major sat astride on a camp-stool and laughed archly.

"I wish I were!" sighed Francis, looking at Eagle. "But, alas! I am no further from bachelorhood than when I saw you last. I saw Phil yesterday."

"Is that the news?" cried the Major, getting grave, and with some tremor in his voice. "Poor Phil! of course you found him at the desk?"

"All that kind of thing is at an end now, Major," said Francis; "and my news is good news, I am glad to say. You and Miss Eagle do not know, I suppose, that Ivy-nook was emptied in haste yesterday, and that the inmates had to fly to London without a moment's preparation or warning, even to old friends here?"

"This is some of your fun, Captain," said Major Marr.

"Not one word of it is fun," returned Francis. "Did you ever hear my father talk of a rich Constantinople cousin of his, a Mr. Beranger? There was some disagreeable estrangement between them."

"Yes," returned the Major, "he used to speak of him, but not very cordially, I admit. Well! what good news hangs on that, Frank?"

"The worst and the best," said Francis; "he died and left the Colonel his sole heir."

"Say that again, Frank—your father the heir!"

The Major's merry face expressed the greatest delight, the utmost satisfaction, as he said this; and Eagle lifted up her bright face wonderingly.

"Yes, Major, my father," said Francis. "Phil knows the whole story; but, as I said before, all this obscurity of his will now be at an end. Bright days are peeping through the Oxford trees; Phil will leave solicitor's work, and enter his name for the bar now—eat his terms—and, some day, turn out a second Mansfield or Eldon, and I hope Florian will make a good wife to him, for he deserves it."

"God bless her, boy! God bless them both!" The Major leaned his head on his hand and finessed away a tear. "But look here, Frank, only between you and me, you know, what if Florian should—should not desire to fulfil her engagement with him now, because she is an heiress!"

"Go to the devil, Major!" cried Francis, hotly.

"Thank you, Frank, thank you—very much obliged for the advice!" said the Major.

"But what the deuce do you think women to be, sir?" cried Francis, warmly. "Here is Philip, who loved my sister when she was poor; he would not form a wealthy marriage for her sake; but toiled and toiled at a laborious profession from morning till night for years,—for her sake—and for yours and Eagle's."

"Yes," said the Major, finessing no longer, but wiping his eyes with a handkerchief. "Yes, it is quite true, Frank."

"He only requires a little incitement and money to make him great and successful in his profession," continued Francis. "And when Florian has become rich, do you think she will desert him? If she does—if she does!" Francis struck his knee angrily; I thought of Florian's words to Philip and trembled.

"It would be a tremendous shock to poor Phil," said the Major, "and to us all. She is his idol, his ambition; he has made up his mind to the marriage, his soul is bound up in her. But don't be so heated, boy, Florian will never behave thus."

"Never!" cried Eagle, facing us with flashing eyes, and all her curls shaking like a bird's black wings. "Florian will never act like this, Papa. I am the only woman here, and the only one that knows how a woman would feel and act; and Florian will marry Phil, Papa, although she were Queen of England! A few thousand pounds don't change us so much; we don't care for money. I would marry Phil, although I should die for it; and so will Florian."

"Bravissima, Miss Eagle!" cried Francis.

The orator bent her head till all her flapping locks hid her face.

"I know you would, Eagle," said her father, proudly.

"And what makes you think that Florian would not, Major?" said Francis, earnestly.

"I don't know, boy, I don't know," said Major Marr. "I'm always afraid of riches. When money gets in among people, it makes sad havoc sometimes; there are no affections, however deep or old, that it does not play the traitor to. But, to tell you the truth, Frank, I don't think, by any means, that the world's wealth would change either Florian or Philip."

"That's all right, Major," cried Francis. "I knew that was the opinion you held, in the bottom of your heart. Here's a letter of invitation for you both to come and reside with us in London. You need not open it; I know what answer to bring back—a 'Yes,' of course!"

"I'll go with pleasure, you sly dog!" said the Major. "But I think it safer to leave Eagle behind me."

"You're a Bluebeard, Major!" cried Francis, "and I, for one, will rebel against your tyranny. You will come with your papa, won't you, Miss Eagle?—or elope with Mr. Gessler and me, to-night, if you like it better?"

"I'll see," said Eagle, with a flirt's toss of the head.

"You will not go away to-night, Frank?" said the Major.

"Bless your soul, Major, I must," said Francis. "I'm absent without leave, and must be on parade to-morrow morning at beat of drum; otherwise Miss Eagle——" (Here the Major struck him playfully). "But, jesting apart, we must be off to London, after we have done that business about Ivy-nook; the Colonel is to give it up, you know."

"And there will be no more whist, backgammon, or Waterloo stories," sighed Major Marr, "not to speak of Florian and Mark. That is one of the pleasures of riches already, Frank."

"You'll all enjoy them together in Blank Street, London," said Francis. "But, by-the-bye, do you know a Dr. Castellon here?"

"The days of wizards and alchemists are over, Frank," said the Major; "and it is superstition, now, to believe in magicians and necromancers, otherwise——"

"You would think Castellon one?" said Francis.

"But really the man is mysterious," continued the Major. "He has a laboratory at the top of the house, where a light burns perpetually; he took me there once. He has a pretty daughter—a fine girl."

"My friend, Gessler, knows the old Faustus," said Francis. "But come away, old fellow; for as we must leave by the first train, we shall barely have time to call on him, the landlord, and Mrs. Stone, at Ivy-nook Cottage."

He rose from his seat.

"Won't you remain to dinner, gentlemen?" said the Major. "We have some choice fish to-day; haven't we, Eagle?"

"Don't tempt us more than we are able to bear," said Francis, "for we must take the wings of the railway, and fly away this afternoon."

So we departed. On our way, Captain Ryder did little else than rhapsodize on Miss Marr's beauty; he had, he owned, been in love, in some sense, a time or two before, but never with heart and soul, as now. He would go back, and propose to her then and there, and let business, the train, and all go to the deuce for him, etc. etc. I mildly pointed out, however, the impropriety of such a precipitate declaration, and suggested that he might as well wait till he had transacted his business and arrived in London, and then make the twopenny postman his Mercury, if in the same mind then as now.

This settled the matter, and eased his lover's anxiety. Then we walked quickly to Mr. Hayes' residence, and passed poor Pietro Wells' dwelling on our way. Thence we went to Ivy-nook Cottage. My pulses beat loudly and hotly as I passed the threshold of Florian's home. The smallest and most common object that met my gaze had a deep interest in my heart; her footsteps, her breath, her former presence, made the very stones in her dwelling beloved and precious to me. Mrs. Stone, a quiet, mild-eyed, bustling, motherly-looking woman, met us; Master Francis was evidently a household idol.

"And you'll never come back again, Master Francis?" said she, when I gave her Florian's card.

"I hope so, Mrs. Stone," replied he; "but Florian will, I'm certain; she wanted this to be our home still."

Mrs. Stone then read her mistress's letter with emotion.

"The cradle's broke, Master Francis," said she.

"What cradle, Mrs. Stone?" inquired he.

"The one Miss Florian wants," she replied. "You was all nursed in it, but you broke it one day, Master Francis, with playing rocking-horse on it. Do you think I should get it mended before I send it?"

"No," said I; "send it in its present state."

"That would be advisable," exclaimed Francis. "Florian, you know, does not actually require it for herself; she merely wishes to preserve it as a relic. But how soon she may require it is another question."

"Always joky, Master Francis," sighed Mrs. Stone. "Bless their hearts, she'll marry Master Philip, of course; and, speaking of them, how sorry the poor old Major will be at your leaving us, dear good soul!"

"And Miss Eagle, Stone!" put in Francis.

"Yes, the pretty love," sighed she. "And Miss Florian won't be married in Oxford after all?"

"I think not," said Francis; "but you will be advised of the event, and must come to see it. Do you think she could get a better husband, Stone?"

"Not I," said she. "Master Philip was quiet-like in his ways, not free and joky like you; but he was as kind and charitable a gentleman as ever lived. They are made for each other. You've comed to a fortune, I hear, Master Francis?"

"So we have, Stone," said he; "you'll hear all the particulars very shortly. How are Mr. Stone and the children—well, I hope?"

"Not so well as usual," said she. "Poor John's took the rheumatics, and Bessie, I'm afraid, is in for the whooping-cough; but Ben is a fine scholard."

We entered the house by a small flower-garden. The flowers were in beautiful order and profusion, some of the creepers climbing the walls and shadowing the casements. The interior of the house bore marks of cultivated taste and straitened circumstances. She led us into the drawing-room; it was well arranged, but the draperies were pale and faded, and the gilding dim and old. Florian's piano, harp, pictures, portfolios, and books were scattered over the room; and on the wall hung an admirably executed portrait of her. She was represented standing beside a rustic gate, in a long, flowing, dark-coloured dress, which fell on the grass, where lay a sketch-book, and a large straw sun-hat. As her head was bent, more was seen of her brow than of any other feature (except her eyes), and her forehead was the most lovely part of Florian's face. The background was composed of foliage; but through an opening in the branches light fell and mingled with her hair. Her small fair hands were crossed upon the gate, and one of them held a few broken wild flowers; the artist had not forgotten to paint Philip's ring on her finger. As a work of art, picture and portrait alike were perfection.

There was another portrait of her, a miniature, when a child, pressing a little dog to her bosom, and laughing through her blue eyes. "Florian, at three years old," was written on the back. There were also several portraits of Francis and Mark, taken at different ages. The likeness of Colonel Ryder, in Captain's uniform, hung over the fireplace; it might have been taken for a stiff, formal one of Francis at a brief, first, hasty gaze; but a close second inspection dispelled the illusion at once.

"You will remember all the directions in Miss Ryder's letter, Stone?" said I. "You will forget none of the articles she mentions?"

"No, no, sir," said she; "you may be sure. Perhaps, Master Francis, you would like to go into that bedroom for the last time."

"No, no, no! Mrs. Stone," cried he, passing his hand over his eyes. "As it is to be scattered and given to strangers, I cannot look at it again."

"Perhaps you will let me enter?" said I.

She gazed at me a moment, and then pushed the door open. It was a bedroom, and a bed with blue damask curtains stood near the window, where branches of honeysuckle swung and waved fragrantly, their shadows lying on the white counterpane. It was on this bed that Florian's mother had died.

"Miss Florian wants to have everything in this room sent her to London," said Stone.

"I am not surprised at the desire," said I. "Is that a likeness of the late Mrs. Ryder?"

The picture represented a benign-looking lady, of pale and delicate beauty, with Florian's features.

"Yes, sir," said Mrs. Stone; "and a more blessed lady never lived; Miss Florian is her born image in everything."

While she spoke my eye had fallen on a half-torn pencil sketch of a simple landscape, and an old tattered pocket Bible which lay on the mantel-piece; they had Florian's name written on them, and they belonged to her; they were useless, castaway things, but I dared not obey the impulse within me, to beg or steal them, as the act would have aroused suspicion of my sentiments towards her; so I restrained myself. We stood silent together for some moments; then she closed the door and I rejoined Francis. He was leaning sadly on the hall window, looking out.

"The Major spoke truly," said he; "wealth has often unpleasant consequences. When I leave this house, poor and unpretending though it be, I shall feel myself, in heart, at least, poor and homeless. I can scarcely tear myself away. I have played with Florian and Mark in that garden, and my dear mother's voice and footsteps echo through the house! Come."

CHAPTER IX.

DESMOND AND SHERRY.—FRANCIS MATRIMONIAL.—
A GHOST.—A PICTURE.

"A spirit of health, or goblin damned."
Shakspeare.

We wended our way through the Oxford streets in almost profound silence. After our visit to Ivy-nook Cottage, Francis became sad and taciturn, and I followed his example, not through sympathy, but from a deeper feeling—even sorrow itself. Every street I passed brought long-cherished hopes to my mind, which no future could now realise; my step became slow and weary, and my eyes turned from familiar objects with pain and disgust. The streets were full of gownsmen. I knew many of them intimately, but I only nodded to them when I could not escape giving some token of recognition. Their gay laugh palled upon my jaded ear. I was no longer a careless young undergraduate, but an unfortunate old-young man, under the weight of a great and irreparable sorrow.

We had just turned into a quiet street, when I saw a chum of mine, Desmond St. Titus, a Balliol man, the eldest son of an Oxfordshire baronet, and heir to a fortune of sixteen thousand a year; indeed, his reversion was about the only possession he had, for his mental capacities were so limited that I doubt if he was ever known to think or reason. He despised anything in the shape of genius, learning, or talent, and in most respects was little better than a fool. He was "plucked" at Oxford, and finally expelled for coarse irregularities out of college and ill-spelt lampoons on the dons in it. Still, he was a good-humoured, harmless, thoughtless fellow, and, on the whole, I rather liked him.

"My dear Des," said I, taking him by the

hand, "how are you? I am truly delighted to see you."

His attention being at the moment riveted by some distant object he did not at first perceive me, but the moment he became aware of my presence he exclaimed,—

"My dear fellow, how you have grown." As soon as he had recovered from his surprise at the supposed increase of my weight and inches, he added, pointing to a vine leaf in his button-hole, "Going out for a lark, Gess, my boy—you twig? Vine is the emblem of—what dy'e call him—Bacchus—isn't it? Sherry and I are going to drink the royal family's health till morning. A regular trump is Sherry, a glorious fellow for a carouse. We wont go home till morning—till morning—till morning!"

As several small libertine boys swelled the bacchanal chorus, I hushed the leader of the minstrelsy.

"Pray lower your voice, Mr. St. Titus," said I; "and don't tread on that old gentleman's toes, he may have gout."

"Gad! Gessy," said he, in a frightful whisper, "that gentleman's the governor; and if he sees me I'm done for." And thereupon he plunged into a milliner's shop. When his venerable sire was out of sight he issued out again.

"Gad! what an escape!" said the heir. "He's off to hear some confounded lecture on the 'Early Christians,' and he'd have me off with him. What a laugh Sherry will have at this! Look at that critter in the blue dress; what an instep and boot! isn't she a duck? Gad! Gessy, introduce me!"

I pleaded my inability, as the lady was quite unknown to me.

"Gessy," he went on, "I'll call for you some morning before breakfast; you twig, eh? just to see you, old fellow, and I'll bring Sherry, too. Where do you hang out?"

"I reside in town," said I; "No. 3, Blank Street, London."

"Gad!" replied he, "I'm going to town myself next week; for I'm in the Line now, old fellow,—in the Buffs,—an ensign, on full pay!"

Francis, who heard the whole conversation, was in convulsions of laughter. He came forward, and, being introduced to Mr. Desmond St. Titus, we all walked on.

"Gad! how the critters stare, old fellows! Nothing like vests," remarked St. Titus, moved to this sentiment by the glances of a group of ladies. "But, somehow, gentlemen, my compliments to women get changed by the air before the critters hear 'em, and they flare up as if I threw eggs at 'em. They think a man capable of originating such vests must look down on 'em, but I don't; I respect every bonnet that's not above ogling the waistcoat!" And he walked beside us with the same inspired feelings that animated Brummel's heart when he wore the first starched neckcloth, only that the Beau thought "starch made the man," but the Buff, that "vests made the gentleman." We met Sheridan Gladmore.

"Ha! here's Sherry, as large as life!" cried St. Titus. "Come here, old fellow! and allow me to introduce you to a man in 'Our's,' Captain Ryder, of the 3rd Buffs."

"Here's three of us, then!" cried Sherry, shaking hands with Francis and St. Titus, "for my commission to that very regiment has been signed by Her Majesty to-day!"

St. Titus imperilled the delicacy of his vest by embracing his dear friend and comrade Sherry.

"Come to my rooms, gentlemen," said Sherry, "and we'll have a night of it together; then the whole four of us can have a run up to town to-morrow morning."

We had to decline with thanks. At parting, Francis invited the two Buffs to his house in town, which invitation they heartily promised to avail themselves of. This may appear a very trivial incident, not worth recording; but, as the sequel will show, it was big with Francis's fate.

"What a fine fellow Gladmore is!" said Francis. "And St. Titus—what an amusing fool! We shall be fast friends in town. Now for the old magician!"

Dr. and Miss Castellon greeted me with great kindness. Kilda had never looked so lovely; her demeanour was almost majestic;

and in her countenance, which was pale, placid, and faultless as that of a statue, there was an expression of sorrow, which became her well. She did not speak much or move often, and her posture did not often change. Sitting in the large deep arm-chair, her white face and hands contrasting with her dark eyes and the gloomy hue of the garments which she wore, she appeared to be much more thoughtful and subdued than usual. How different was her manner from that of the last lady we had visited—the bold, bright, laughing Eagle, with her rosy cheeks, ceaseless motion, and tossing curls. They can never be rivals, thought I. A complete transformation seemed wrought in Francis. He had become silent and thoughtful; all the easy and fascinating gallantry which characterized his manner to women had disappeared; his flow of small talk was stopped, and he sat twirling his hat, or toying with his gloves and cane, leaving all the conversation to the doctor and me, for Kilda was also silent.

"Your father wishes to collect all his old and early friends in his house in London," said Dr. Castellon. "He is kind enough to call me an old friend, and sends me an invitation. Certain duties connected with my scientific studies, prevent me from accepting it at present; but as the invitation extends to my daughter, she can go."

Francis bowed without uttering a word, and Kilda's eyelids fell.

"I know Colonel and Miss Ryder will feel great happiness in meeting Miss Castellon," said I. "Shall I tell him that you intend to follow her?"

"No, I will write to him," returned the chemist, gravely.

"Is Madame Castellon at home?" interrogated I.

"No, she is not at home," said Castellon.

"Have you heard of Colonel Ryder's accession to a fortune?" said I. "The fortune of his cousin who died yesterday."

"Albert Beranger dead!" exclaimed he, in a tone expressive of deep regret. "Was it sudden? Nay, I need not ask, it must have been so."

"No," replied I, "he gave premonitory

symptoms long before his death; he seemed to anticipate the end his illness would have."

Dr. Castellon's eyes grew troubled, he fixed them on me.

"Were you in the house when he died?" said he.

"I was," answered I, "in the very room itself a moment after."

"Was Madame Castellon in the house when he died?" he inquired.

I paused in extreme embarrassment. I did not wish to betray Madame if I could help it, and I shrunk from the necessity of falsehood.

"You have not replied to my question," said Castellon, a cloud gathering on his brow. "Was Madame Castellon in that house when Albert Beranger died?"

"Yes."

Kilda moved uneasily, and Castellon muttered to himself.

"How many physicians attended him?" said he.

"Only one," replied I, "Dr. Mustapha from Constantinople."

"Did a friendship or intimacy appear to

exist between Madame Castellon and Dr. Mustapha?" inquired he, anxiously.

"They appeared to be anything but friends," answered I.

"There seemed more friendship between her and Beranger?" said he.

"Not much there either," replied I. Castellon drew a deep breath.

"Did any interview take place between her and the Colonel?" said he.

"They never met. She left the house as the Colonel entered it." Kilda listened breathlessly.

"Beranger had a ward or *protegé* in the house, I believe?" said he. I bowed. "Did she seem friendly with him?"

"Very," replied I, anxious to escape from this searching inquisition.

"Very!" echoed he. "Kilda, you will accept my friend's kind invitation, and you will tell your father this, Mr. Ryder. You are very like your father, sir, at least in form and feature; do you think there is a mental and moral resemblance also?"

"No!" interrupted I, hastily. Castellon smiled.

"You are in haste to get out that 'No,' Mr. Gessler," said Dr. Castellon. "Pray pardon me, but I must now leave you, gentlemen; the chemist is a slave. Good morning."

"I think you are changed since I saw you last, Miss Castellon," said I.

She rested her brow upon her hand and replied,—

"You are mistaken, Mr. Gessler; I do not feel myself changed,—and there is no change."

"You do not possess your usual vivacity," said I. "You are paler, more silent and grave, than formerly."

"I am only more natural," replied she. "I now let my true self appear, without an effort to mask or to improve it. When I was gay, I was only an actress."

She laughed musically, and said,—

"But you are changed, Mr. Gessler, and for the worse, too, for you were never false or flattering before!"

"My faults have begun with you, then," said I.

"And you have never flattered a lady since you left?" said she.

"Not one," replied I, colouring.

"Nor will not when you leave again?" interrogated she.

"No, Miss Castellon."

She rose from her chair; a little bird began to pipe lustily outside the window,—

"Shame that thrush, Miss Castellon," said I, "and give us a song."

Without a word she sat down at the piano. As I laid the music-book for her she said in a low voice,—

"Why did you betray my mother's secret?"

"To save myself from falsehood," said I. "You saw that."

"Is it not as great a crime to infer false things, as to speak false words?" said she, severely.

"Are you angry with me?" said I, earnestly.

"Not with you," said she, "but with your ideas of falsehood and truth, candour and duplicity; for they are wrong, Mr. Gessler, very wrong."

My answer was hushed by a dashing prelude, which melted into a soft foreign aria, with Kilda's voice breathing and tinkling through it here and there. Then the music ceased.

"Is this your song, Miss Castellon?" said Francis.

"Yes, Captain Ryder, my songs are all songs without words: I leave my hearers to supply the poetry."

"Like the little bird that sung on the ivy?" said Francis.

"I have no sympathy with the insipid music of a bird's song," said Kilda, "for it is nothing but joy from beginning to end. Give me the murmur of the sea-shell, the lash of the ocean, and the rush of the wind. These have strength and passion, sorrow and regret, in their tones. I do not care for melody and softness; but for the language, the thought. Although I do not understand Italian thoroughly, I like to hear operas, for how easily I can translate the tones of a Jenny Lind, a Grisi, and a Mario!"

"Sing another song without words, then!" said Francis, "and let me try and translate it when it is done."

She trilled several wordless cantatas, and Francis translated them; under his breath, however, that I might not hear him. The whistle of the train at this moment reached us.

"It is easy to translate that sound," said I.

Francis rushed to his hat, cane, and gloves; and bidding farewell to Kilda, we took our departure.

Francis, who was generally loud and eager in the praise of every woman who could call one charm her own, was silent on the subject of Miss Castellon.

"So," said I, "you do not admire Kilda so much as Eagle?"

"What the devil makes you think that?" said he, sharply.

"Because you have not said one word in her praise," replied I.

"Hem! Walk quicker, old fellow, or the train will be away."

"No fear!" exclaimed I; "plenty of time yet."

"And why did you make me run away in that headlong manner?" said he, "if there is plenty of time?"

"Pray, do not be so snappish, Captain," said I. "You will see her again in London, you know."

"Who, Gessler?" exclaimed he; breaking down branches with his cane.

"Eagle," answered I, wickedly. "How will you write your proposal to her to-morrow morning before breakfast?"

"Ah! yes," said he, "Eagle is a glorious creature, as fresh and open as a young violet; but love is like a fever, you know; we may catch it unexpectedly at any moment, and sometimes lose it as suddenly, for, thank goodness, there are a great many cures for it!"

"Oh! no," said I, "love is as slow and

gradual as consumption, and ends like it, in death!"

"Gessler!" exclaimed Francis, earnestly, "I may jest and banter as I like, and seem as volatile and fickle as the vane turning on that church-steeple there, but I believe this is love too, as you have defined it just now. I begin to think seriously on marriage at last, for the man who has not some true, pure, loving woman bound to him is an unhappy man. Not to be loved by woman is a misfortune, but not to love woman is a crime!"

"That is all very true," exclaimed I, sighing, with a desolate yearning in my heart. "Very true indeed."

"My mother died," continued Francis, gravely, "and now the last tie that binds me to woman is breaking, for Florian is to marry; and after that——"

"There can be no other tie!" said I, bitterly.

"You forget a wife, old fellow!" exclaimed Francis. "There can be no home without a woman; so give me your advice, prejudice apart, should I marry?"

"By all means," answered I; "but whom will you marry?—Eagle, of course."

"Whom I will marry, is not the question," said he, looking confused. "Should I marry? tell me that, and I'll soon get all the other matters arranged."

"If there is not a woman whom you feel better in loving, one of whom you could never dream an evil or harsh thought, one whose influence purifies your spirit, and whose example stirs you up to the performance of good deeds—if you do not know a woman like this, *never marry!*"

"Here we are at the station," said Francis, interrupting me; "go and get the tickets."

"It is not necessary," said I; "I took return tickets at the London side."

"Bless my soul! so we did; I quite forgot!" cried Francis; "my bad memory has lost me many a pound."

I saw all the things from Ivy-nook Cottage safely deposited in the luggage train; they were invaluable to Florian, and I watched them with jealous care. Then we steamed away from Oxford. It was the delight of my existence to be with Francis, because of his wonderful resemblance to his sister; he was better than any painted likeness of Florian, for he reminded me of her not only in feature but also in tones and motions, ay! even in heart and mind. Alas! alas! why must love, the romance of life, so often have the dark ending of tragedy? On our return to London I found Pietro Wells dressed as for a journey, with some books thrust under his arm.

"I'm going away, Mr. Gessler," said he, "back to Oxford. I am obliged to you for your great kindness to me, but do not press me to remain here longer. Albert Beranger is away, and there is another master here, a man whose bread and salt I would not eat even if I were a starving beggar. So you see I must go."

"You will get no train to Oxford to-night, Mr. Wells," said I, "so you must rest contented for one day yet."

He did remain, very unwillingly, however; and next day he fell ill of a fever, during which he raved and tossed, muttering continually in his strange foreign tongue, so that even delirium kept his secrets safe; for his nurses, Florian and I, could not understand a word he uttered, except such familiar names as those of Albert Beranger, Mercia, Edmond Ryder, Mustapha, Castellon, Rome and Constantinople. Florian, who with the tenderness and kindness of a ministering angel adhered to the letter and spirit of medical prescription, took the poor usher all to herself. As he lay in one of my apartments, this threw us into perpetual contact, and thawed the coldness of reserve which honour prompted me to assume towards her. But her presence was a sunbeam, and the ice around my heart was gradually melting away. But frequently memory would place the form of Philip between me and the rapture of which I was dreaming, and I would ask myself the question,—"Shall I foster and encourage my love for Florian, till the very moment when she stands beside the altar with Philip?" That were indeed madness, dishonour, and crime.

As I had now begun my duties of tutor to

Mark, I fulfilled my promise to Mr. Tamper, and wrote him a short note acquainting him with the fact of my engagement. Mark and I progressed marvellously well as teacher and pupil. But he had one defect,—he wanted application to a single study at a time; he had not half conquered one difficulty when he would fly away to overcome another; he had only mastered the first lesson in Latin accidence when he wished to plunge into the difficulties of Greek. This fault was caused by too much of the imaginative faculty. But despite all this, my first pupil was the best I ever had; his physical debility impeded us considerably, it is true, but application at other times made up for the interruption. Here too I was thrown into Florian's society; we met daily, hourly; I was only a man; have some consideration, then, for all I did and felt, and spoke and suffered!

Major Marr, Eagle, and Miss Castellon arrived, and then the house and its inmates became the gayest of the gay. The Colonel gave a round of dinners, suppers, balls, and *conversaziones*, and old friends who had apparently forgotten his existence crowded in. He received cordial invitations from every part of the three kingdoms. The veteran and the young military flocked round the father and son; and gambling, betting, hunting, carousing, and luxury in all its shapes and forms, lured and enticed the fortunate sons of wealth. Sherry Gladmore was Francis's dearest and most intimate friend; they were never separated at home or abroad, by night or day. Florian received several proposals of marriage from handsome and dissipated rakes; men of rank and fashion, but whose morals and reputations could ill bear the light. Some of them were poor, fortune-hunting scoundrels; and others rich sensual villains, or wealthy brainless idiots. How the very sight of Florian's lovers used to make me shudder! The best of all her admirers after all was Desmond St. Titus; although his intellect and habits were none of the best.

Before proceeding further, I will lay the substance of Mr. Tamper's reply to my letter before the reader, a reply which, while amusing me, mortified in no small degree my *amour propre.* After praising the succinctness of my style, as he was pleased to phrase it, he complimented me on the excellence of my handwriting. Digressing thence, he told me that I possessed admirable qualities for a good lawyer's clerk (cool rather all this, thought I), and that, as he would need some one to take in time Philip Marr's place, he would, out of his great regard to myself (this was put in the most insufferably patronizing manner, or so at least it seemed to my vanity), receive me into his office, first in the capacity of copying clerk, and afterwards as time passed, should I—and he doubted not I should—prove myself able to discharge the duties expected of me as general manager in his absence. He added, moreover, that if I was ambitious, he knew few better ways of rising in the world than that suggested; referring to several well known members of the Bench and the Bar, who, beginning life as drudges in attorneys' offices, had afterwards been able to enter their names for the higher profession at one of the inns of court, and so, owing to the practical knowledge acquired in early youth, had risen to eminence by the time they arrived at middle age, &c., &c. He then favoured me with some of his own peculiar views of life, cynical, worldly-wise, and of course utterly selfish, reminding me of nobody so much as Goethe's Mephistopheles in a patronizing humour; and so ending with wishes for my welfare—signing himself in true attorney fashion—

"Yours (without prejudice)

"M. TAMPER."

I fell into a reverie over this letter; and the colour—the fate—the end of my whole life, quivered in the thoughts of that moment.

That night a strange incident occurred. The ladies had retired, the domestics were asleep, and save myself and a card party in the dining-room, consisting of Colonel Ryder, Major Marr, Francis, and Sherry Gladmore, no one was out of bed in the house. The Colonel's bedroom was near mine, and as I often heard him go out and in during the evening, I thought nothing of it when I heard him enter on the present occasion, till a loud cry and a heavy fall, apparently proceeding from his room, struck upon my ear, and I immediately rushed in. The Colonel was lying back in a chair, his limbs quivering, and his white staring face covered with perspiration. Visions of sudden death by apoplexy and heart disease passed through my mind, and I grew fearfully alarmed.

"Water! air!" cried he, in a hoarse gasping voice, as I came near him. "For God's sake, water!"

I was going away for some, but he grasped me by the arm.

"Do not go," said he, trembling. "Let me have flesh and blood near me. For your life do not leave me!"

"But the water," said I. "Pray let me ring the bell, it is only across the room."

"I tell you," exclaimed he, vehemently, "that all the life, health, and water in the world could not repay me for the horror of a moment's loneliness! Stir not, I tell you!"

I remained quite still, marvelling at his words, which were an enigma to me. At last he pointed to some dark object at our feet.

"Take that up," said he, hastily, but do not let it touch me; show it to me, but keep it off!"

I raised it up, and found it to be the strange picture which Baptist had painted for Mr. Beranger.

"Mercia! Pietro!" cried he. "It was he then after all; wine and fancy did not delude me. The dead walk the earth, and I am haunted! Curse the sin and the ruin of a wanton's love! I worshipped her, but I curse her. Hide her from my sight!"

His form swelled with passion, and I covered the picture. He wiped his forehead, and rose to his feet.

"I am a soldier," said he; "I have been in the thick of battles, at the front of forlorn hopes, at the cannon's very mouth; I have done what the bravest of men have hesitated to attempt, but (and he smiled bitterly) I am afraid to go downstairs to-night without the protection of a school-boy!"

I took the hint, and walked to the door without a word; at the same time thinking that a schoolboy might be morally braver than a man who had been in "forlorn hopes," for the Colonel was a believer in the supernatural, and the so-called "schoolboy" was not.

"I once 'winged' a man in Madrid," said he, with another bitter smile, "for calling me tipsy; but I will feel obliged to you, Mr. Gessler, if you tell all who ask you about this scene, that I have been so to-night; but you would favour me more by being totally silent on the subject."

Here the hero of forlorn hopes started at a white curtain which fluttered in a dark room; and the distant banging of a shutter shaken by the wind seemed to freeze him with horror. We reached the dining-room door, and voices sounded within.

"Halloo! Sherry," cried Francis, "you've won from me again. Whatever colour you choose, you are sure to win."

"Well, then," exclaimed Gladmore, "let us cut *rouge et noir*, and play dice. Mine are always lucky."

"Yes, to yourself, Sherry, I daresay," said

Francis, "but not to me, I never won at dice with you in my life."

"Take some more claret, old fellow!" cried Gladmore; "the more wine the more luck, they say. Throw first."

"I say, Frank," said Major Marr, "I would advise you to stop playing more this night, you've lost enough already. Men should not drink wine when they play for money; either give up the playing or the drinking. Look at Mr. Gladmore."

"You flatter me, Major," cried Sherry; "I've drunk more wine than the two of you put together."

"It did not throw you off your balance, then," said the Major, "for you are clear-headed enough yet."

"Do not play more, Frank," said Gladmore; "for the Major is certain that you'll lose."

"Yes, I will play till I am victor," cried Francis. "The cards again, Sherry—fifty on the red!"

At this juncture the Colonel bid me "good-night," the door closed, and I heard no more.

But this snatch of conversation made me thoughtful and troubled. Sherry Gladmore had once been suspected, at Oxford, though the charge was never proved, of loading his dice, and of using marked cards when he played with novices and strangers; might he not so impose upon Francis? Thoughts like these, and others as dark and perplexing, so occupied my mind when I retired to rest, that even in sleep I continued harassed by the troublesome dreams which they suggested. When I went to the studio next day I found Baptist lying exhausted upon a couch, but even amid the weariness of flesh and spirit, his eyes burned with their usual lurid and restless glare.

"Where has that gaunt old bookworm gone to?" said he—"Wells, I think you called him—I miss him, for he seemed to dislike me; he made me one of his books too, and I have seen him, when he thought himself concealed by the shadow of the curtains, peering curiously at me, as if he would read my every word, look, and action. I wonder if he understood what he read in me?"

"He is confined to his bed with fever," said I. "Poor man!"

"Poor, indeed!" exclaimed Baptist; "for his conduct to me was that of one who possessed neither truth nor honesty. What does he rave about?"

"I do not know," answered I, "for he speaks in a strange language."

After musing a moment, Baptist inquired abruptly—

"Do you hear anything more of that marriage?"

"Miss Ryder's?" answered I; "no, but it will take place, I suppose, at the time appointed."

"Florian looks wan, pale, and unhappy," exclaimed he. "What is the meaning of it? Does she love this man—this Marr?"

"I will be truthful with you," said I; but pray do not repeat what I say; I know that she does not love Philip Marr."

"Then in God's name!" cried he, starting up, "why will she marry him?"

"For honour's sake," said I; "they were affianced before."

"Pooh! We are not to break our hearts for honour's sake. I have little acquaintance with Marr, but I think him a man of honour and good feeling; he surely possesses more self-respect than to gain a bride by coercion; he will give her up."

"No," said I, "I know him well; he is not only a man of deep feelings, but also of stubborn will. I know he is resolved to keep her to his claim. Both I and Miss Ryder have tried to shake his determination, but our efforts have been useless."

"Have you pleaded together?" asked he, with some irony.

"No,—apart," answered I, colouring to the temples.

"You are disinterested, Gessler," cried he; "you incur the anger and suspicion of your friend, for the sake of this strange young lady. Beware!—suspicion from both parties may be your reward."

"Philip Marr does not suspect me," said I.

"If I were in your position, I would rather that he did."

"You speak strangely, Baptist," exclaimed I.

"And you look strangely, said he. *I* suspect you."

"Of what?" My heart beat loudly and wildly.

"Do not practise the cowardice of hypocrisy," exclaimed he, sternly. "You love Florian Ryder—you covet your friend's affianced bride. Hush! not a word, your looks, your words, have already betrayed you."

"I will speak," cried I, excitedly. "If I feel as you say, if it is dishonour so to feel, I am dishonourable against my will; the feeling existed long before I knew of the betrothal to Philip."

"And did Florian know of its existence?" said he.

"I never uttered a word to her on the subject, or she to me," said I. "But excuse me, Baptist, you take a marvellous interest in Miss Ryder's affairs; I have a right to suspect you also." I spoke bitterly.

"Yes," replied he, after a pause. "Florian and I love each other; but it is with a calm, passionless love which makes me neither Philip Marr's rival nor yours; you need not be jealous of the feeling with which I regard Florian. While we are on the subject tell me this, does young Ryder mean to make Kilda Castellon his wife?"

"I think so," said I. "Though you may think him vain and variable, Captain Ryder is a noble fellow."

"So is Gladmore," said Baptist, "that wine-bibbing scoundrel; if he treats me as a boon companion again, and addresses his vile wit to me a second time, I'll kick him. The inseparable friend of such a man must indeed be a noble fellow! I intend going to Rome shortly."

"To Rome!" echoed I, in amazement.

"Yes. No true artist could die without seeing Rome. As I have few friends or enemies here, I will leave England without pain, with Art for my companion and Nature for my tutor."

"Your last picture, the 'Giaour,' created a great sensation among the artists of London," said I. "I hear its praises everywhere."

"Oh! yes," said he, contemptuously. "Fashion has accorded me a season's reputation, but do you imagine that glory? No!" cried he, passionately. "I have toiled and will toil for something greater; I am not famous, but fashionable. I would rather be hissed at by hate and envy, than be the sleek pet of silken patrons in their gilded saloons. My ambition aims at something more lasting than a season's immortality."

He grew pale with vehemence, and as footsteps were heard approaching, I said nothing more to him.

Florian immediately after entered the room; and going up to Baptist, she put her hands on his brow.

"How feverish and throbbing it is," said she. "You work too hard, Baptist, dear; I never thought that these beautiful pictures, which I admire so much in the galleries, were the produce of toil, fever, and, I had almost said, agony. If the idea had occurred to me, I could not have looked upon them with so much delight. The works of Art seemed so beautiful, that I never thought of the labour by which they were accomplished."

"But this toil," cried Baptist, "is the

artist's existence. I knew a poor artist once whose sight became impaired, in consequence of his enforced idleness. He grew mad in a month, and raved about his colours and his brushes. Come and look at my picture."

He brought a picture with the tints yet wet on it, and placed it in a good light; the subject was King Lear and Cordelia. The features of the fiery old monarch were grand and noble; anger blazed in his eyes, and scorn was seated on his lips. Cordelia stood before him, in her simple, loving pity, holding out her childlike hands, and lifting up her fair face in sorrow and wonder, scarce realizing the fact that she was repelled by her aged father. And the original of this beautiful conception, as a single glance was sufficient to show, was Florian.

"Oh!" cried Florian, "you are not a good portrait painter, Baptist, for you have made me beautiful; now I own that I feel, or could feel, like Cordelia, but I have none of her loveliness."

"The likeness is very striking," said I, warmly.

"It must be Cordelia's white satin dress and pearls then," said she, simply, "that make her look so lovely—so much better than I."

"I tell you, Florian," cried the artist, eagerly, "that when you stood for my model, with your hair flowing and your arms stretched out and bare, you were the perfect likeness of this. Artists say that fidelity of portraiture is my forte."

"So it would appear from this picture," said I. "It is so like life that one could almost fancy it breathed, or was about to step from the canvas. And that is the great triumph of art, is it not?"

"No," said Baptist. "The greatest triumph is to touch the passions. Could you shudder at that old man, and weep for that girl? That is the question. I painted a puppet once, so natural that a child on seeing it screamed with laughter. That Dancing Jack was a masterpiece; it sold well."

"I shall not add a touch to this picture," said Baptist. "You have ceased to be Cordelia. How shall I pay you for the favour of this sitting?"

"With that picture of dear Eagle," said Florian.

"Why," said Baptist, "it is a mere sketch. I intended it for the head of a young gipsy; but take it; the arch minx will give me another sitting."

"Thank you, dear Baptist," said Florian. "You will come down this evening to our quiet little family music party? There will be no strangers."

"Except Mr. Gladmore, I suppose," said Baptist.

"No," smiled Florian, "he will not be here to-night."

She placed her hand on his arm, and her face was so near to his shoulder, that when he turned he could have seen the throbbing of the slenderest vein in her eyelids. But I felt no jealousy; for this fond familiar affection of Florian's, made me love Baptist the more.

END OF VOL. I.

CPSIA information can be obtained
at www.ICGtesting.com
Printed in the USA
LVHW100441110522
718424LV00003B/184

9 783375 006877